1/13

X

The Cadence

Of

Gypsies

Barbara Casey

The Cadence

Of

Gypsies

Barbara Casey

An imprint of Gauthier Publications

Gauthier Publications
P.O. Box 806241
Saint Clair Shores, MI 48080
Attention Permissions Department

This is a work of fiction. All characters in this book are
fictitious and any similarities are coincidence and unintentional.

1st Edition
Proudly printed and bound in the USA
Hungry Goat Press is an Imprint of Gauthier Publications
www.EATaBOOK.com
Cover design and layout by Elizabeth Gauthier

Library of Congress Control Number: 2010941357

With my love,
For Sophia Belle,

Who dances to the cadence of gypsies ...

Kud ce vjestica do u svoj rod?

(Where should a gypsy* go if not to her kin?)

—Old Gypsy Proverb

As their peculiar perfume is the chief association

with spices, so sorcery is allied in every memory to

gypsies. And as it has not escaped many poets that there

is something more strangely sweet and mysterious

in the scent of cloves than in that of flowers, so the

attribute of inherited magic power adds to the romance

of these picturesque wanderers. Both the spices and

the gypsies come from the Far East—the fatherland

of divination and enchantment. The latter have been

traced with tolerable accuracy. If we admit their affinity

with the Indian Dom and Domar, back to the threshold

of history, or well-nigh into prehistoric times, and in all

6

ages, they, or their women, have been engaged, as if by elvish instinct, in selling enchanting merits, peddling prophecies and palmistry, and dealing with the devil generally ill a small retail way. As it was of old so it is today—

Ki shan I Romani—

Adoi san' I chov'hani.

Wherever gypsies go,

There the witches are, we know.

Gypsy Sorcery and Fortune Telling

Charles Godfrey Leland, 1891

*Gypsies were often considered witches. In many instances the word, "vjestica" was used interchangeably to define a witch and a gypsy. The original translated quote uses the word witch.

Chapter One

The gypsy—not old, but beyond her birthing years—spent the early, pre-dawn hours digging roots in the dark of the crescent moon, every so often replanting a good piece of a root to grow next year. The day before she had picked herbs, during that time when the essential oils are at their strongest, before they could get evaporated by the midday sun. She had her favorite place where she searched, the place where the energies were strongest. Surprisingly, it was the old church graveyard built on a slight mound just outside of the rural Italian village of Frascati. A creek ran nearby, and a tall, unkempt yew tree grew near the entrance to the graveyard, poisonous, but giving off positive energies. It was a place she knew well, having discovered it from a previous time the travelers came this way.

Other gypsy women picked their herbs anywhere they were found, or they would buy them dried from a shop, claiming good results. But *Kaulo Camio*, a black gypsy who went by the name of Lyuba, knew better. To capture their full spiritual healing essence, she treated all plants kindly and with respect. For she believed as good gypsies did that everything has a spirit, even the stones on the ground, and everything could bring luck—good or bad.

Once she had gathered her herbs, she returned to camp just beyond the village to prepare her potions. From the roots, bark, and hard seeds she would make decoctions by soaking them overnight and boiling them the next day. To some of the decoctions, she would add honey or sugar; to others she would thicken into syrup or add lard to make ointments and salves. She saved the freshest herbs for her oils.

Soon her potions would be ready, and she would take them into the village to sell. Coughs or colds, rheumatism, cuts and bruises, burns—it didn't matter. She knew how to relieve pain, create lustrous hair, revive the impotent, whiten teeth, cure constipation, or simply heal the broken spirit. Unlike others who only pretended, she had the gift.

But that would be tomorrow. Today, after her work was complete, she would teach the children. Lyuba was a *choovihni,* a wisewoman, an exalted and envied position among gypsy women. As her birthright, she alone was given the responsibility to pass on the knowledge of the travelers to the ones who would follow. Today she would teach the older children about spells, making the *duk rak* and *duk koor* for protection, as well as the talisman. This particular group of children was bright and eager, but she had yet to find a child born with the natural gift. Those children were rare. In all her years as a *choovihni,* she had only known one—the beautiful one that was taken from her so long ago. All of the magic she knew could not heal her pain from that loss.

Outside her hut, the shadow of the elm was short; the sun almost directly overhead. She needed to finish for soon it would be time for the children. She carefully placed the last of the herbs in a bottle and covered them with olive oil. Sealing the bottle tightly with a cork, she put it with the others where it would be gently warmed by the sun.

* * *

Jimmy Bob Doake didn't like change. Born and reared in Piedmont, North Carolina, and the only sibling out of eleven to make it to the eighth grade, he never felt a desire to visit or move to anywhere else. He still lived in the house where he grew up, at least during the day, alone, except for his hound dog, old Tick. He spent his nights only a couple of miles down the road at the Wood Rose Orphanage and Academy for Young Women, his place of employment for the past 30 years. This night was no different.

Jimmy Bob slowly made the rounds in his old beat-up truck, starting with the outer perimeter along the ivy-covered stone walls surrounding the campus. He gradually circled his way toward the middle of the large, wooded property until finally reaching the center where the administration building was located. Without fail, the entire process took him two hours and 43 minutes. However, on those nights when his favorite team was playing on television—it didn't matter which sport—he would only patrol around the dormitory and the administration building, which would take 15 minutes.

Since there had never been any reason to change this routine, he would always leave his office to go on patrol at midnight. And because Jimmy

Bob was a bit of a poet, often spending his solitary nocturnal hours transferring his inner-most thoughts onto paper while others slept, he visualized himself as heroic, charged with the weighty responsibility of keeping all safe during those hours he referred to in meter and rhyme as "witches' moments"—the magical time that occurs between late darkness and early light.

Stone apparitions, familiar and functional in daylight, now seemed unfamiliar and somewhat threatening in the soft illumination of the crescent moon high overhead. Everywhere dark, elongated shadows crisscrossed the lawn dampened by night-cooled air. The stillness was broken only by the rhythmic croaking of frogs from a nearby pond, an occasional splash, a mocking bird off in the distance, and the slight rustle of leaves.

Though the favored Durham Bulls had gone into extra innings against the Indianapolis Indians, the minor league baseball game was being televised by the local station in a delayed broadcast, therefore eliminating the need for Jimmy to cut his patrol short this evening. At exactly two hours and 43 minutes after he started his rounds, he parked his truck and entered through the locked door of the administration building, located on the east end.

Within minutes he was comfortably reinstalled in his over-sized recliner, positioned in front of the 12-inch television he kept in his small office. It was the top of the 15th inning; the Bulls 6, the Indians 5. The Indians were up to bat. Next to the recliner on a small table was a bag of cheese chips, a canned soft drink, and the pad of paper and pen he kept handy just in case he felt inspired to write something—a word, a phrase, a nice couplet.

All was as it should be.

* * *

"Ouch! You're standing on my fingers!" said the petite girl with a long, blond ponytail. Her nightgown was pulled up between her legs and tied into a knot at her waist to keep it from getting tangled on the limb where she was perched. Somewhere above her the sound of a saw and splintering wood filled the darkness followed by a stream of profanity repeated in several foreign languages for emphasis.

"It doesn't look right. It's supposed to have a rim and a dent," said the heavy-set girl with a slight lisp. She was wearing a nightshirt buttoned at the neck, and clinging to a 12-foot ladder as she pointed the flashlight.

The petite girl with the blond ponytail giggled.

"What do you mean—*dent*? Let me see that picture." The completely hidden, tall black girl aimed her flashlight toward the magazine being thrust upwards through the thick branches in her direction.

"And the top is supposed to be rounded—like a button mushroom," the girl in the nightshirt added, the word "mushroom" sounding more like "muthroom."

"That's because it's circumcised," supplied the girl with the ponytail, as she removed a small twig and a handful of leaves from the magazine.

"*Shekoo, baboo!*" More profanity. "Okay. I know what to do." The tall black girl disappeared back into the upper-most branches of the tall plant that was more tree than bush. After several more minutes, the sawing, crunching, and clipping sounds finally gave way to the more gentle sounds of tiny snips. And then, silence.

"That's it; everybody down."

With the magazine that had been overlooked in the last confiscation wedged firmly under her armpit, the petite girl started the perilous descent first since she was nearest to the ground, followed by the tall black girl. The girl in the nightshirt eased her way down the ladder last, juggling pruning shears, a hand saw, and scissors. Once on the ground, the three girls stood back to admire their work.

"That is one honkin' *Peni erecti*," said the tall girl, causing a fresh explosion of giggles. "Let's get out of here." After quickly rolling down the legs of her pajama bottoms, the tall girl grabbed one end of the ladder and, along with her two friends, lugged it and the other tools back to the shed that housed lawn maintenance equipment. Task accomplished, they returned to their rooms, careful not to disturb the other dorm residents, the floor monitors, their suitemates and, most important, their slumbering dorm mother, Ms. Larkins. Within minutes they fell into a deep, peaceful sleep—the sleep of innocent angels.

It would soon be light, and Wood Rose Orphanage and Academy for Young Women would start another day.

Chapter Two

It was always the older ones who felt the need to challenge the ancient gypsy traditions. The children who weren't yet adults, but who felt they were old enough to thwart authority and desire independence.

"I want lots of gold," said Milosh, who had recently turned 17 years old—a man in his opinion. The oldest in the group, soon he would join the adults. "Teach me the spell to make me wealthy."

"You must be careful for what you wish, Milosh." As always, the *choovihni* was patient with her young pupils. "But I shall teach you the spell for attracting material goods." She sat in the shade of the tall elm with her full skirt spread out around her and waited until everyone was quiet and settled before continuing. "First, write down whatever it is you desire on a clean sheet of paper, then place the paper on a small square of green cloth. You must concentrate on it for a few minutes. That might be hard for you, Milosh," she teased. The other students laughed. They liked for Milosh to be put in his place. Just because he was the son of the Bandoleer, it didn't make him better than everyone else, even though he acted like it. He played mean tricks on the younger ones who were too timid and afraid to say anything. "Try to visualize the object before you—the shape, texture, color. Feel pride in owning it, the pleasure you hope it will bring, what you will do with it." She looked at each of her students, making sure they understood. "Then hold the paper to your forehead and say three times: 'I have you, I hold you, I keep you.'

"Fold the paper into the green cloth and tie it with a length of red wool. Tie seven knots into the wool and as you tie each knot, say, 'You are mine, I own you.' Put the green cloth with the paper in a small box, and each day, for seven days, hold the box to your forehead and say three times, 'You are mine, I own you.' After you have done this, put the box away in the back of a drawer."

"Will I have lots of gold if I do that?" Milosh asked.

"It will bring success to those who are patient and deserving," Lyuba answered.

For the next several hours, Lyuba taught the children other spells: the spell using the power of trees, a ritual to cleanse the aura of their individual spaces, the spell for strength. When they got older, she would teach them spells for attracting romance and for keeping a loyal lover. For now, however, she would teach only those things that were appropriate and what they could understand.

When the day's lessons were complete, and the elm's shadow once again lengthened, the parents came for their children. Concerned, Lyuba watched Milosh return to his hut alone. His *chakra*, that point of light indicating the heart, was dark and brown rather than green as it should be. Much was expected of the only son of the Bandoleer. He held promise, but he had much to learn. Unlike his father, he was impatient and quick to judge others. His focus was on material things, and he ignored what was important. There was also a darkness in his spirit; something that could be dangerous if not corrected.

He would go and prepare the paper, wrapped in green cloth and tied with a thread of red wool, and wish for much gold. He had not understood.

* * *

The slight voice tremor was all that was needed, but the deep, audible sigh confirmed what Carolina suspected: she was in for another real ass-chewing. This was her eighth time called into the headmaster's office in the same number of months since she had been teaching at Wood Rose Orphanage and Academy for Young Women. Each time it had been because her girls had either committed a serious infraction of rules or behaved in some inappropriate way, which was unacceptable within the stone walls of Wood Rose.

Her girls, the ones she had been given total responsibility for, called themselves Females of Intellectual Genius, or FIGs. Everyone else, however, called them strange. Never before in the history of Wood Rose had a student even come close to approaching genius status. Certainly not in the time that Dr. Harcourt had been headmaster. Then, within the short span of one week, two seven-year-old children—Dara Roux and Mackenzie Yarborough—were admitted, each from a different family, a different background, and a different part of the country, but each with an intelligence quotient well within the range of genius. Amazingly, several years later, a third student was enrolled. Jennifer

Torres's age and scores were comparable to those
of the original FIGs. What Wood Rose could do for
these gifted girls was now coming to a close, much
to the relief of the administration, faculty, and
staff. This would be their final year at Wood Rose,
for in June—less than six weeks away—they would
graduate.

Carolina was still in bed, deep in thought,
when the telephone rang. For several days she had
been struggling with how best to approach the
headmaster. Shortly after getting hired at Wood
Rose, she was put in charge of the FIGs. Since then
she had tried to devise innovative ways to excite her
girls, challenge their intellect, and, most of all, keep
them out of trouble. The inherent problems of being
different extended beyond their prickly relationship
with Wood Rose staff members. The multi-faceted
difficulties in teaching the FIGs frequently left the
faculty with feelings of inferiority and impotency.
None of the other residents wanted to be around
them either. Only the youngest residents, who
didn't yet comprehend the difference between being
brilliant and normal, sought the FIGs' attention.
This brought about additional struggles of an inner
psychological nature. Carolina had tried a variety of
approaches, but, obviously, what she had been doing

wasn't working. What had stimulated her when she was their age? What mysteries of the universe had intrigued her?

Then she remembered.

She had just turned 18 when she was accepted into the accelerated liberal arts program at the University of North Carolina in Chapel Hill. That summer, in preparation for the fall term, Carolina was assigned an extensive and comprehensive reading list. That was when she made the discovery, and from that day forward, her life and the way she thought of herself had been charted in a veil of mystery and immeasurable conjecture. What if … became her mantra. She felt as though she had been thrust into a parallel universe. Nothing had excited or concerned her more, before or since. It became her own secret research project, something she remained totally committed to—even with a heavy class schedule that would guarantee an early graduation from the university. It was what motivated her to get up every morning and what kept her working late into the night. With each new bit of information, no matter how small or seemingly unimportant, she was pointed in a different direction, to another amazing discovery and thrilling revelation.

The dedication to her search had not

diminished in the years since she first made her discovery. In her personal analysis of it, she didn't know what she hoped to accomplish. She only knew she was somehow connected to one of the greatest mysteries in the world by some strange twist of fate. She also recognized that it was her responsibility to seek an outcome, for, in the end, it would define her very existence.

Within three years of being accepted to the university, Carolina graduated *summa cum laude* with a bachelor's degree in liberal arts; and then, because she didn't know what else to do, she earned a master's degree in foreign languages, and a doctorate in psychology. Through it all, the secret remained with her, her special project. Like an invisible companion, she chipped away at the hidden truths. By staying closely associated with the university, she could access research materials that would otherwise be difficult or even impossible to obtain, especially when it involved materials from foreign countries. It was her obsession, consuming all of her spare time between classes, assignments, lab work, and whatever else was necessary to fulfill graduation requirements. It was her best friend.

There was Larry, of course, who was more than a friend. He was the one person she shared everything with and who had been amazingly helpful in her search for the truth. But other than Larry, she didn't have many friends. She certainly did not have the kind of friends she could ever confide in—about this. And the tenuous connection she had felt with her adoptive parents as a child had all but dissolved once she went off to college. Now, there was only the project. The knowledge that it was a part of her sustained her. It was her mission in life, until, abruptly, one day the real world came into focus.

Her adoptive parents had been more than generous when funding her education, but now, "We have retirement to consider," they patiently explained, "and since you are 25 years old with a doctorate degree ..." She needed to get a job.

Of course they were right, and Carolina immediately applied for a position with the institution where she had spent the last seven years. Because of her outstanding educational qualifications, she was hired as an assistant professor of psychology with the university, teaching many of the courses she had just completed. Three years later, she learned of a unique employment opportunity at Wood Rose, located 20 miles from Chapel Hill in Raleigh, and without a moment's hesitation she sent in her application and resume. Maybe it was her background and the uncertainty of her origins that made her want to teach at the orphanage. Or maybe, after spending so many years in Chapel Hill, she simply felt the need for change. The only difficult part of her decision: She wouldn't see Larry every day. "But we can talk on the phone," she had told him. "And we'll have weekends." He had said he understood.

Naturally she was hired. She was young, energetic, highly qualified, and trained, and someone, the headmaster hoped, who could handle the FIGs during their final year at Wood Rose. Certainly, no one else could.

With the time-consuming pressures of adjusting to a new job, and the FIGs in particular, and getting familiar with her different surroundings, Carolina's personal research project got put aside, temporarily tucked away like a rare, precious treasure to be rediscovered on another day.

And it was. It was so obvious. The FIGs were the brightest students at Wood Rose; in fact, they were in the top two percent of the entire population, according to their intelligence quotient scores. Each girl had unique qualities and talents that would be perfect for what Carolina had in mind. Although the academic program at Wood Rose was excellent, these girls needed more than the education offered to them, Carolina reasoned. They needed a challenge, especially before they left the protective environment of Wood Rose. Carolina wanted to give them something special they could take with them— something that would be a source of strength to them for the rest of their lives. It was then that Carolina took out her treasure and examined it to make sure she wanted to share it; and, deciding that she did, started putting together a plan.

Considering the many implications, analyzing all of the repercussions, anticipating the negative questions she would receive and her responses, she thought she had worked out all of the details and was just about ready to make an appointment with the headmaster to discuss it. As she lay in bed thinking, the early morning light softly filtered through the newly-hung blue paisley draperies she had recently sewn, and she was reminded of the Robert Browning poem she had always loved:

> *The year's at the spring*
> *And day's at the morn;*
> *Morning's at seven;*
> *The hillsides dew-pearled;*
> *The lark's on the wing;*

The snails on the thorn;
God's in his heaven—
All's right with the world!

Presenting her plan would be delicate because it meant doing something totally out of the norm for Wood Rose. It meant breaking with routine, and if she had learned anything since arriving at Wood Rose, it was that no one went against the fixed and steadfast regime that had been entrenched at Wood Rose ever since it first opened its doors. But if she approached Dr. Harcourt at just the right time, and could get approval from the board members, and Miss Alcott, of course, perhaps ... Then the phone had rung.

"Ms. Lovel ... I need to see you in my office—immediately." The sigh had followed.

She grabbed her appointment diary, which she kept on the nightstand next to the bed, almost knocking over the small milk glass lamp in her haste, to see if she had forgotten something. It was Sunday and, therefore, no classes were scheduled. There was only the usual routine: a brisk two-mile walk with her girls at 7 A.M., followed by showers and dressing, and then breakfast at 8:30. Mandatory chapel services for the student-residents were conducted from 10:00 A.M. until 11:00 A.M.; faculty and staff were also encouraged to attend, but it wasn't required. Carolina chose not to. She preferred to use that time to think of ways to stay at least one step ahead of her three charges. The rest of the day would be spent in the library helping the girls—not that they needed it—finish up their term paper. She had assigned a report on Mary Shelly's motivation and inspiration behind her character of Frankenstein. It was an assignment the FIGs had enjoyed working on together, and they had uncovered some interesting information. When completed, their report would probably be good enough to get published in one of the literary journals. They would take a break at noon for lunch, and again at six o'clock for dinner. Lights were out by 10 P.M., even on the weekends.

A superior academic program, routine, discipline, and the much-maligned dress code— an assortment of required clothing for outer wear, under wear, and sleep wear appropriate for recreation, classrooms, and chapel, which varied only slightly according to the age of the resident—created the foundation on which Wood Rose Orphanage and Academy for Young Women had been built. In 1894, the founding fathers had insisted on it, and from then until now it suited those who financially supported the orphanage.

The Methodist Church was one of the largest supporters, with an annual contribution that more than adequately took care of 35 percent of the administrative costs. A representative from the Methodist Church sat on the Board of Directors along with 11 other members from the community— mostly successful business leaders—whose combined donations totaled another 14 percent. These board members, reverently referred to as the 12 disciples by those who lived and worked at Rose Wood, also organized an annual Christmas fund-raising charity ball. The proceeds were donated to the orphanage for expenses not covered in the budget, such as landscape beautification, or local field trips when deemed appropriate.

In addition, each year Wood Rose was awarded several State grants, which were earmarked for special educational programs. There was also the occasional donation from individuals who wanted to "help the poor little dears."

Finally, there was Miss Edna Grace Alcott, the feisty 87-year-old great niece of Horace Alcott, a tobacco farmer who had originally endowed the orphanage in the late nineteenth century. She contributed the remaining funds necessary to keep

Wood Rose running successfully. In recognition of her continued philanthropy and generous spirit, the chapel had been given her family name: Alcott Chapel. A large portrait of Miss Alcott hung next to an equally large portrait of her uncle, both done in oils, in the vestibule above a Queen Ann console table. Centered on the table where it could be observed each Sunday before services was a Waterford crystal vase filled with pink roses, something Miss Alcott had requested since the pink roses complimented the pale pink color of the garment she wore in the portrait. Without fail, these roses were replaced with fresh ones every Saturday morning; another request.

Dr. Thurgood James Harcourt had served as headmaster at Wood Rose for 27 years. During his tenure, enrollment had remained fairly constant, ranging between 38 and 40 residents, as it had since the beginning. Only during the height of the Depression did enrollment skyrocket to more than 100 students. During his first 12 years as headmaster, he proudly maintained the proper image of Wood Rose, which was expected of an institution affiliated with the Methodist Church. Although nothing remarkable occurred during this time, nothing improper occurred either. Then the first two FIGs arrived. Adjustments had to be made; certain challenges met. The newest young residents had difficulty fitting in with the other, already-established residents. Therefore, soon after their arrival the administration determined the FIGs would be happier if their rooms were located near one another in the same suite. An extra floor monitor was also assigned to help watch after the high-spirited girls with exceptional minds. Then there was the ongoing challenge of developing an educational program to meet their intellectual needs. Often this extra work created discontent among the faculty, and feelings of inadequacy.

Negative press, which had never been a problem prior to the girls' arrival, now seemed to be a constant threat. This could result in smaller donations, which would mean the difference between meeting budget needs, or reducing the already limited number of faculty positions.

When the third FIG arrived only a few weeks before Carolina assumed her new post, other adjustments had to be made and different challenges met, causing Dr. Harcourt to question whether it was worth having three intellectually superior residents full of *joie de vivre*. All of his efforts to maintain a positive, dignified image of Wood Rose with the press and the community at large over the years now occasionally took on a carnival atmosphere because of the FIGs.

However, the slightly stooped but otherwise healthy 59-year-old headmaster with gray thinning hair had no desire to retire early. He had managed to keep the reputation of Wood Rose unsullied, and he did so with firmness and decorum. No one was more dedicated or intimately involved in the detailed operations of the orphanage than Dr. Harcourt, and no one took greater interest in its success. The dark gray suites he wore, the conservative gray-striped ties that might give way to a smidgeon of maroon on special celebratory occasions, and his stern demeanor were a reflection of the rules of strict discipline and unwavering routine that had been passed down to him from previous headmasters suited his nature.

The way Dr. Harcourt had emphasized each syllable in the word *immediately* when he called Carolina, however, and, of course, that sigh, suggested the routine was going to be changed on this particular Sunday morning, and that "all was not right with the world." The reason undoubtedly being that the three young women Carolina was personally responsible for, her FIGs, had once again done something unbelievably disrespectful, impertinent, unmindful of authority, border-line destructive—and utterly amazing.

Chapter Three

Milosh prepared the bundle. The single word *gold* was scrawled on a sheet of paper, wrapped in a square of green cloth his mother had given him, and tied with a length of red wool. He rapidly repeated the words, "I have you, I hold you, I keep you," until he grew weary. Lyuba had said he must put the bundle in a box and repeat the words for seven days. He wouldn't wait. Instead, he shoved the bundle to the back of a drawer and went outside. It was getting dark and already the elders were sitting around the campfire. Milosh's friends were seated there as well, just behind the elders in the shadows, where they could listen but not be observed. He sat down next to one of the boys, pushing a younger boy out of his way. The younger boy did not challenge him.

As usual the talk began with incidents that had occurred that day.

"There have been many changes since the last time we passed this way." The Bandoleer opened the conversation.

There were murmurs of agreement. "It is no longer a small village," said one of the women, who had spent the day in Frascati.

"There are more people, but fewer want to buy," said another who had also spent the day trying to sell her services, but had little to show for it.

"We must be patient," said the Bandoleer. "There are many who don't know we are here yet. When they find out, they will want what we have to offer."

Lyuba remained silent. She hadn't wanted to come back to Frascati—not yet. There were too many unhappy memories here. But it hadn't been her decision to make. More often than not they were getting turned away by the settled population. There were fewer places for them to go. Estrangement was causing distrust, and distrust resulted in fear of the travelers. "They are from the lost continent of Atlantis," some of the settlers said. "They are the last of the priestly caste of the old Egyptian religion, forced out by the New Order," said others. There had even been an archaeological study done linking the DNA between present-day European gypsies to the ancient tribes from India. The settled people didn't understand what the gypsies knew: There have been travelers since the beginning of time, and there would be travelers until the end of time, no matter what the *gorgia* believed.

Lyuba had been especially watchful since their arrival, anxious that she might be punished for her actions so long ago. It was the one time she used the dark magic. Even now, after more than 25 years, she didn't regret it. She reached into the fold of her skirt and felt the small stone worn smooth by the river. It had a tiny, natural hole in it; it was her lucky charm. That morning while she had been digging roots, she had made a small offering—a hair pin—in the nearby stream before returning to camp. She asked for the blessing of good fortune in this place that caused her so much pain.

* * *

"It sure didn't take long for him to notice." Jennifer flipped off the hair dryer, quickly brushed her long blond hair, which was still slightly damp, and pulled it back into a ponytail. Dara and Mackenzie were already dressed in uniforms appropriate for Sunday services—dark blue skirts, yellow blouses, black pumps, and blue tights—and were sitting on Jennifer's bed. "What do you think he'll do?" She walked toward the door as she tied a dark blue ribbon around the rubber band holding her hair in place. The other two followed.

"Not much," said Dara. "What can he do? We will be out of here in a few weeks."

"He might decide not to let us graduate," said Mackenzie.

Dara raised her eyebrows. "Not likely. Do you really think Thurgood wants us around any longer than necessary?"

The three girls skipped down the flight of stairs and hurried out of the building. It was just a few minutes past seven when Mrs. Ball, Dr. Harcourt's administrative assistant, had called to tell them the headmaster wanted to see them. They had showered and dressed in record time. No need to make him wait any longer than necessary. Outside they crossed the lawn, ignoring the Do Not Walk On Grass sign, and paused briefly in front of their artistic creation from the night before, silently paying homage— except for Mackenzie who giggled—before entering the administrative building. Mrs. Ball was waiting for them when they got to her office, located just outside of the headmaster's. As before on similar occasions, she provided no verbal or physical indications that would reveal what they were in for.

"You girls may be seated. Dr. Harcourt will be with you momentarily."

The three girls sat in the same chairs they had previously sat in when called to the headmaster's office. Dara sat closest to the wall, both feet firmly planted on the floor, knees together, looking straight ahead. Mackenzie sat next to Dara, pulling at her skirt as she crossed her legs. And Jennifer, turning at an angle toward Mackenzie and Dara, moved her chair ever so slightly, scraping the floor when she did. Mackenzie fluffed her short brown hair and giggled, and then coughed in an attempt to cover up the act of slight injudiciousness. Dara simply continued to stare straight ahead. Mrs. Ball frowned at all three of them and then continued sorting through the paperwork on her desk.

"She has the hots for Thurgood," Dara whispered to the other two.

Once again there was the scrapping of the chair and a spasm of coughing until, under the pointed glare of Mrs. Ball, all became quiet.

* * *

Carolina quickly showered and dressed. As a member of the faculty, she lived within the stone walls of the orphanage property in her own one-bedroom bungalow, something for which she gave thanks every day. Before coming to Wood Rose, she had lived near the university campus in an efficiency apartment with shared walls, shared noises, and shared smells. Now she only had her own walls, her own noises, and her own smells, which were a combination of fresh citrus and herbs, and whatever else was in bloom that she had brought indoors. She loved her little house, and the privacy and independence it afforded, even if it was a bit like living in a fish bowl. After all, there wasn't much distance between the dormitory and the bungalows. On more than one occasion since her arrival to Wood Rose she had sensed she was being spied on. She even thought she saw binoculars poking out of a second-floor dormitory window where the upper-class residents, ages 15 through 18, lived, aimed in her direction.

Still. She took special pride in her bungalow, lovingly decorating each of the small rooms in an Italian provincial style, with happy colors of blue and yellow and splashes of burnt orange. The bungalow had come sparsely furnished, but Carolina, using the sewing machine borrowed from fellow faculty member Dr. Dolores Smythe, an expert in international affairs, geography, and politics, had worked wonders with slip covers and cushions, a few throw rugs and, most recently, draperies for her bedroom.

And outside, on the little plot of land where her house squatted, she added to the boxwood hedges and single camellia bush those things she knew would thrive in the Piedmont soil of North Carolina: daffodil bulbs, azaleas, and forsythia bushes in anticipation of spring; hydrangeas and pyracanther with its red berries for the hot summers and autumn. It was her own touch, and it gave her bungalow a slightly different appearance from the others; better attended.

Landscaping was something the previous tenant had neglected, either out of laziness or because of other interests. She guessed the latter since she had been quietly informed by one of her colleagues, Dr. Frank Sturdavant, a professor of math, calculus, and statistics, that the man had been released from all duties a short two months after he had been hired. Apparently his lifestyle was in direct opposition to the morals and teachings Wood Rose was trying to instill in its all-female students. This last bit of information had been revealed through a twitching lip and one profound snort.

Carolina owned a white Honda Civic, but she rarely drove her car unless it was to go into town to shop for incidentals such as fabrics for sewing, or a few groceries for those times when she needed a break from cafeteria food, or if she felt the need to explore somewhere beyond the walls, in which case she usually took the FIGs with her. Except for Larry, everything that was both necessary and important in her life existed within the walls of Wood Rose. Her project, of course, was a different matter; its boundaries were still undefined.

The administrative building was an unadorned three-story stone behemoth centered on 60 heavily-wooded acres of donated land. Radiating from the administrative building in a semi-circle, much like the ribs of a fan, were two, two-story buildings, also built of stone. One contained the classrooms accommodating grades one through 12. The other was the dormitory where 38 orphans, ages five to 18, lived. Each floor was divided into several spacious multi-roomed suites, the residents assigned according to class: elementary, grades one through six; middle, grades seven through nine; and high school, grades 10 through 12. Located in perfect juxtaposition between these two buildings and completing the semi-circle, were three, single-story stone buildings that housed the library, the cafeteria, and the infirmary.

Beyond the stone buildings, surrounding the perimeter of the property were various maintenance buildings. And scattered amidst the bucolic, pine-wooded landscape were the individual bungalows where the full-time faculty lived, one of the contractual requirements that went with teaching at Wood Rose. Faculty members had to live on the orphanage property in the housing provided. All staff, however, lived off the orphanage property except for the dorm mother, Ms. Larkins, and the headmaster's secretary, Mrs. Ball. She had moved into her bungalow only a few years earlier, shortly after her husband died, with the full approval of Dr. Harcourt, the Board of Directors, and Miss Alcott.

There were 10 bungalows in all, each constructed in white clapboard with gray slate roofs, with a comfortable layout that gave the on-campus residents the option of cooking in their own kitchens or eating in the cafeteria. Dr. Harcourt and his wife lived in the largest bungalow, of course, which had two bedrooms. Other faculty members with spouses also lived in two-bedroom bungalows, although theirs didn't have as much square footage as the headmaster's or as much landscaping. The single faculty members and Mrs. Ball were given the smallest, one-bedroom bungalows, and Ms. Larkins, a single woman, had a private suite in the dormitory building.

"Did you see it?" Elizabeth Humphry, a professor of English literature, Romance languages, and art history, asked. She practically knocked Carolina down when she rushed out of her bungalow to meet Carolina as she passed.

"See what?"

Elizabeth's eyes widened, emerging above the round, black-framed glasses she wore to correct a bad case of stigmatism and near-sightedness. Shaking her head in disbelief, she hurried back into the safe environment of her bungalow, closing the door with exaggerated determination.

What could they possibly have done now? Even though Dr. Harcourt hadn't revealed his reason for summoning Carolina, it never even occurred to her that it was anything but something her girls had done. Last month, they had wrapped Dr. Harcourt's pristine office in aluminum foil. Everything—pens, sheets of paper, curtains, desk, rugs, telephone—was covered in silver. Even the paperclips piled in the black-veined onyx bowl, a gift from another graduating class, were each individually wrapped. Nothing had escaped.

Punishment had been light, considering it was their latest creative expression, as it was referred to around campus, in a long line of inappropriate, disruptive behavior they had subjected Dr. Harcourt to over the years, probably because he realized they would be graduating and leaving Wood Rose soon. The FIGs were ordered to unwrap everything and then confined to their dorm rooms for two weeks other than going to the cafeteria for meals, or to the chapel for Sunday services, which was pretty much their usual routine anyway.

The month before that it had been the discovery of unauthorized reading material—or, more explicitly, magazines revealing male nudes—in the FIGs' rooms. Contraband of this nature was totally unacceptable, stringently opposed to the morals and teachings at Wood Rose, and an extreme violation of the rules. For that, they had been assigned kitchen duty for two weeks, washing dishes and cleaning up the dining room after each meal. The symbolism in this punishment had not gone unnoticed by the FIGs or Carolina.

There had been many other expressions of creativity over the years, deeds that had been dutifully recorded in the historical archives at Wood Rose, but lately these expressions seemed to have taken on what most of the faculty and staff considered a more menacing tone of a sexual nature.

Carolina hurried along the brick pathway, bordered by late-blooming tulips and early-blooming peonies, which snaked between the library and infirmary toward the administration building. Up ahead she saw several other faculty members, the early-morning walkers and joggers, standing in a group whispering among themselves. They were all facing in the same direction and appeared to be staring at something. Carolina's heart quickened. Though it was the end of April, the temperature made it feel like summer. Even so, Carolina felt a chill. This was not good. She took a deep breath, attempting to prepare herself and get control of her emotions.

As she approached the others, someone noticed her and, like in the biblical story of Moses parting the Red Sea, everyone silently stood aside making room for her to pass. There, in front of the administrative building, or to be more precise, in front of Dr. Harcourt's large, multi-paned window overlooking the grounds, the dormitory and classroom buildings, the library, the cafeteria, the infirmary, the bungalows, and the maintenance buildings beyond, the headmaster's prize red-tip bush, his *Photinia fraseri,* which stood more than 14 feet high and had a circumference of 32 feet wide; the bush that he had personally fertilized and watered, treated for a rare mold disease, nursed back to health from an equally rare fungus, and hand-trimmed weekly since first planting it when he was named headmaster at Wood Rose, was now pruned to a magnificent, perfectly shaped, 14-foot-tall phallic symbol. A few of the red tips had been left at the top, delicately snipped to create the appearance of a slight red blush.

Carolina's first reaction was to laugh. After all, it really was quite amazing. Just the idea of accomplishing such a fete was something to admire. How on earth had they trimmed the top like that? How did they even get up there? But she soon came to her senses; after all, she was being observed by her peers. She had already been introduced to the hidden jealousies, petty competitions, and downright mean-spirited actions of some of the faculty; she couldn't be too careful on how she conducted herself.

She hadn't been at Wood Rose as long as the other faculty members, and she could very easily find herself dismissed just as Dr. Frank Sturdavant, the former professor of math, calculus, and statistics, had been for inappropriate behavior. She still might be dismissed if Dr. Harcourt held her responsible for this latest violation against him personally, and Wood Rose in general. Just when she had wanted to discuss her plan with him. There was no doubt as to who had committed the sacrilege, and the timing couldn't have been worse. Not wanting to make matters any more difficult by delaying the inevitable, she made her way unhindered through the heavy double-wooden doors leading to the headmaster's office.

The FIGs were already there, neatly dressed in their uniforms, seated in the three chairs lined up against the far wall, just as they had been arranged for previous infractions. Each of the chairs was touching the other, as though linking them would give the girls additional strength. Only Jennifer's chair was slightly off kilter, not quite in line, but touching nonetheless. Like before, Dr. Harcourt would deal with them after he had dealt with Carolina.

They each looked up expectantly at Carolina

when she entered the office. She winked. Then she turned her attention to the sweet scent of lavender and quick, capable movements of Mrs. Lilian Ball, who was transferring some papers from a desk drawer to the file drawer behind her desk. With the last paper properly filed away, Mrs. Ball noticed Carolina and, without saying anything, critically assessed the jogging shorts, t-shirt, and tennis shoes she was wearing. Carolina had brushed her dark, shoulder-length hair after dressing and twisted it up off her neck with a clip, something she usually did whenever she was in a hurry. The look on Mrs. Ball's face made her wish she had done more. Mrs. Ball pursed her lips. "Dr. Harcourt is expecting you. You may go in."

Carolina had been trying to get into Mrs. Ball's good graces ever since arriving at Wood Rose. But for some reason she just couldn't seem to get it right around that woman. Mrs. Ball had been a fixture at Wood Rose even before Dr. Harcourt had been named headmaster. She knew all of its secrets, but Carolina was willing to bet she would never reveal them. Carolina was also willing to bet that if Mrs. Ball didn't like a member of the faculty, Dr. Harcourt didn't either. Carolina's attempt at a confident smile fell a little short as she entered the headmaster's office, which smelled heavily of wood wax and Mrs. Ball. She heard Mrs. Ball close the door firmly behind her.

Mahogany-paneled, thickly-carpeted, and enveloped in dark green fabric, the headmaster's office always made Carolina feel like she should whisper, or maybe bow her head. She wasn't even Catholic, yet she felt the overpowering need to cross herself and kiss her thumb as she had seen others of the Catholic faith do. Perhaps even genuflect. He remained seated behind his desk and didn't expend any energy on small talk.

"I have been more than patient with those girls," Dr. Harcourt said, turning his back to Carolina to face the book-lined wall behind his massive desk. "I have tried to take into consideration the fact that they are ... different, exceptional." This time he spoke toward the sofa that was covered in heavy dark green brocade. "I had even convinced myself—obviously a serious lack in judgment on my part—that by making them your responsibility, these acts of abomination would cease." He shuffled a stack of papers and slammed them down on his desk. "But this is unforgivable!" This was aimed directly at Carolina causing her to flinch. She decided to take the sympathy route.

"Believe me, I understand. I am just so sorry."

He wasn't finished. "I have never seen such a demonstration of insubordination." His breathing was rapid and his face contained a rosy flush not unlike the top of the *Photinia fraseri,* Carolina couldn't fail to notice. She tried another tactic.

"I believe I have read somewhere that it is healthy for large, older bushes to be pruned occasionally. It encourages new growth and keeps them healthy." She smiled weakly.

"Pruned?" He stood up and flailed his arms toward the dark green brocade draperies that flanked the large window now flooded with morning light since the 32-foot girth of leaves and limbs was no longer there to provide shade. "They might as well have dug it up! Burned it! Chopped it down! What were they thinking?" He sat back down, defeated.

This was getting nowhere. Carolina made a quick decision. She would explain her proposal now and just hope that he would agree. At least it would get the FIGs out of his hair, what little there was of it, for a few weeks. Without waiting to be asked, she eased herself down on the edge of the straight-back chair facing Dr. Harcourt's desk, knowing that if she didn't she would probably collapse.

"I think I have a solution. It is educational,

it will give Wood Rose a certain amount of international prestige, it might qualify Wood Rose for additional State grants, and it will keep them away from you for the remainder of the term until graduation." When Dr. Harcourt didn't say anything, Carolina continued. After the first 10 minutes and still no response from Dr. Harcourt, she wondered if he was even listening. When she finally finished presenting her case, he stood, leaned forward, and said two words: "Do it!"

Chapter Four

The FIGs were the latest in a long line of residents to become graduating seniors at Wood Rose. Excluding the faculty, Ms. Larkins, and Mrs. Ball, and, of course, the headmaster, they were among the oldest residents living on campus. Although there were seven other girls who would also graduate in June, without question the FIGs were the brightest and most promising of any students Carolina had worked with as a teacher. Carolina felt blessed. She knew she had been given an opportunity that few teachers would ever get. It was also a tremendous responsibility.

There were three of them: Dara, Mackenzie, and Jennifer. Dara and Mackenzie had been living at Wood Rose since childhood. Jennifer arrived when she was 16 years old, shortly after her parents had been killed in an automobile accident. She had been at Wood Rose for not quite a year, perhaps considered a short time for some, but not for most who called Wood Rose home due to circumstances over which they had no control, and certainly not for Jennifer.

Shortly after Carolina's arrival, it was determined Jennifer should also be included in Carolina's small class because of her exceptional musical and artistic talents. The entire Wood Rose faculty had fully approved and was much relieved by this decision. Each of the girls had an extremely high intelligence quotient, which had been a little daunting to Carolina when she was first assigned the task of looking after them. "They seem to listen to you, Ms. Lovel," Dr. Harcourt had explained. "For whatever reason, you inspire them. Therefore, I am putting you in charge of these girls. I trust you will not fail them—or Wood Rose." From that time on, Carolina had defined which academic areas she wanted each girl to focus on, playing on their natural abilities and talents. She also arranged their recreational activities, which she involved herself in as well. She made sure they were eating properly and getting a good night's sleep; and, in short, she became a big sister to them. Much to the horror of the other faculty members at Wood Rose, she asked them to call her Carolina.

Carolina understood what Dr. Harcourt was saying. She didn't have the IQ of a genius, but she definitely felt a strong bond with these particular girls. For one, she wasn't that much older than they were—an advantage she had over the other faculty. And within a relatively short time after taking on the responsibility of teaching them and being their mentor, she knew she had gained their respect and, perhaps, affection.

Part of the reason, Carolina felt, was because she understood what it was like to be different. She also had been raised by people who were not blood relatives. Growing up, she was given love and comfort and discipline—all of the usual things children need and crave to grow into healthy and productive human beings. Yet, from the beginning, she knew—or felt—something wasn't quite as it should be. Maybe it was the formal manner her adoptive parents treated her; or maybe it was because there was never any laughter in the place she called home.

The summer she turned 18 she learned the truth, or at least some of it. She had been taken from her biological parents just before her fourth birthday and put in a foster home. A short time later, she was adopted by the Bransons. Her biological parents traveled a great deal, she had been told, and couldn't take care of her. She remembered nothing, but suspected there was more to the story. Either no one knew, or they just didn't want to tell her.

Carolina appreciated the things her adoptive parents had done for her and the obvious sacrifices they had made on her behalf, but she never felt the bond she imagined children should have with their parents. The knowledge that they weren't her real parents had strained what little substance there had been in their relationship as parent and child. The distance that had always existed between them became greater.

That summer before she started college, her adoptive parents gave her a sealed wooden box to open. Inside were her birth certificate and some other documents, and a black and white photograph of a man and a woman. There was also a small drawstring pouch—a gypsy *parik-til* or blessing holder she later learned—that contained dried herbs, a small stone, a feather, and a folded piece of paper. Carolina also learned that a savings account with $50,000 had been set up in her name at the time of her birth. Giving her this information at this time was in accordance to the agreement reached between the adoption agency and Carolina's birth parents.

Carolina didn't do anything with the box and the things in it for the longest time. She simply wanted to touch it, hold it close, and take comfort in the fact that she now possessed actual proof of her birth and her real parents' existence, and that they loved her enough to want to provide for her.

When that no longer became enough and curiosity set in, Carolina began her search. She started with the photograph. There was no way she could date it, but it looked as though it had darkened with age. There was nothing especially remarkable about the man and woman in the photograph, except that Carolina looked nothing like them. They wore clothes that were plain and not particularly stylish—perhaps foreign-made. They both had dark hair, dark eyes, and dark skin. The woman in particular looked exotic, with long, dark hair, a full mouth, high cheekbones, and a glimmer of laughter in her eyes—or was that Carolina's imagination?

Then Carolina started researching the names on her birth certificate. Her own name had certainly been a curiosity. Not Carol or Caroline, but Carolina. She had always reasoned that perhaps she had been born in North Carolina, and that was why she had been given such an unusual name. Her birth certificate, however, stated she had been born in Italy.

The names listed on her birth certificate, identifying her mother and father, were even more curious. Her mother was *Lyuba Hearne (Rossar-mescro) Lovel;* her father *Balo (Camlo) Lovel.* Carolina didn't even know their nationality. Eventually, with Larry's help, she found out. Her parents were gypsies. That was when she legally changed her name from Branson to Lovel, the name of her birth parents. Her birth name.

Chapter Five

Milosh hastily pulled the box from the back of the drawer and peered inside. Nothing was there except for the scrap of paper. There certainly wasn't any gold. Disgusted, he crumpled the piece of paper and tossed it back into the drawer, not even bothering to put it into the box. *Lyuba is getting old*, he thought. *She can't even remember the simple things.* He went to the trunk where his father kept things of importance and began to rummage. He had remembered seeing a book about curses. That was what he really wanted to learn—how to put curses on those who stood in his way. On the bottom of the trunk, under a folded blanket, he found what he was looking for. The book was old and tattered; most of it Milosh couldn't even read. But there were parts of it he understood, and the drawings helped. He sat in the corner of the small trailer that had always been his home, positioned now in the shadow of the Old Villa, and studied. Lyuba doubted him, but he would show her. He would show everyone who didn't respect the son of the Bandoleer.

* * *

Except for the white cotton undergarments, which were bought from the discount store in bulk to fit all sizes, the clothing provided at Wood Rose was either dark blue or pale yellow. The class uniforms worn by the girls in high school consisted of a pale yellow blouse that was worn with a dark blue skirt, unlike the yellow blouses and blue jumpers worn by the girls in elementary and middle school. All of the Wood Rose girls were required to wear dark blue socks and black, lace-up shoes until they reached high school. At that time they could do away with the dark blue socks and black lace-up shoes and either wear blue tights with black pumps or, in the hot summer months of July and August, black pumps without tights. The class uniforms were also worn to Sunday services.

In addition to the class uniforms, the residents at Wood Rose were supplied shorts, t-shirts, and tennis shoes for gym class and recreational activities, coats and gloves for cold weather, rain gear for inclement weather—all dark blue and pale yellow—and, of course, the white under garments. Dr. Harcourt and the members of the board believed that by providing uniforms for the residents, feelings of jealousy over clothing was eliminated, and the girls' focus could be turned to more important things, such as academics. In spite of the inflexible rules regarding the dress code, the FIGs had found ways to demonstrate their individuality through the subtle ways in which they wore their uniforms.

Dara, an African American from a back-bay area of Richmond, Virginia, was the tallest and also the most outgoing of the three FIGs. She could speak and write seven languages, including the ancient language of Sanskrit. She always wore her pale yellow blouse with the first two buttons open, thus revealing more of her skin than was necessary in the opinion of the faculty, staff, and administration.

Mackenzie, on the other hand, was a little on the heavy side and had a tendency to lisp whenever she got nervous. Known for her accomplishments in physics, calculus, computers, and problem-solving—especially in the area of complex geometrical puzzles—she wore her blouse with all of the buttons closed. There was no record on file indicating where she had been born or who her parents were, a fact that would make no difference when years later she would be nominated as the first female presidential candidate of the United States.

The newest member of the FIGs, Jennifer, was a petite blond, whose special abilities included art and music composition. She chose to express her individuality in a different way altogether: She didn't wear underwear. Of course, this wasn't as obvious as the buttoned or unbuttoned blouses, but she knew she didn't have any underwear on, and so did the other FIGs. Identified as "a problem child with little prospect for adoption," she had been sent to Wood Rose by an agency in upper state New York.

The three uniforms, and the girls wearing them, stood separated from Dr. Harcourt by his massive mahogany desk. Having read many books on character development and personality disorders, and considering himself an expert in most matters involving the human psyche, Dr. Harcourt naturally noticed the unbuttoned blouse worn by Dara. She was, in his educated opinion, narcissistic, believing the world revolved around her. The buttoned blouse worn by Mackenzie, an obvious display of anxiety paralysis, only confirmed his belief that she suffered from paranoia. He wondered what he was missing when he glanced at Jennifer. She was probably a borderline personality with a tendency toward violence. In any case, he decided their slight dress code modifications weren't worth mentioning. He didn't mention the *Photinia fraseri* either. Instead, he merely instructed the girls to go to breakfast, then to Sunday services. "Ms. Lovel will talk to you later and explain *things*," he said. As soon as the three girls left his office, he broke out in song, alarming Mrs. Ball to the extent that she immediately called security.

Carolina's suggestion had made him almost lightheaded. For the first time since the FIGs had become residents at Wood Rose, he felt he might actually be freed from the frequent migraines they had caused him over the years. Not only would they be off campus and out of sight, they would be out of the country and, therefore, unable to cause any additional turmoil and destruction at Wood Rose.

Naturally, he had heard of the Voynich Manuscript; it was one of the great mysteries of the world. Apparently, Ms. Lovel had not only heard of it, she had spent several years researching it, something, oddly enough, that had not been mentioned on her resume. He wondered why. Her proposal to involve the FIGs in her research, however, was a good one. In fact, it was brilliant. It would certainly challenge their intellect. And, if anything came of it, there was the strong possibility that it would lead to additional State funding for Wood Rose. Ms. Lovel had even offered to pay for their expenses while abroad, to which he agreed; and because it wouldn't involve an additional strain on the budget, he didn't even see the need to get advance approval, which might delay their trip, from the Board of Directors. Not even from the outspoken Miss Alcott.

Standing slightly to one side of the multi-paned window, and partially hidden by heavy green fabric, he watched two men, part of the crew responsible for taking care of the grounds at Wood Rose, struggle to put the severed limbs and leaves hacked from his precious *Photinia fraseri* into several large black plastic bags. He had told Ms. Lovel to immediately start making whatever plans were necessary. As soon as she had everything finalized, she was to leave a copy of her itinerary with Mrs. Ball. Naturally, this study abroad mini course, which is how she described it, would conclude in time for graduation. But not before, he was quick to add. He wished them much success and would look forward to reading their findings.

Being completely honest with himself, he was a little envious of Ms. Lovel and the trusting relationship she had managed to build between herself and the FIGs in such a short time. As a former teacher himself, and as chief administrator of an educational institution, he only wanted what was best for the student-residents. He wanted to see each girl develop to her fullest potential and succeed. But he knew that he had fallen short with the FIGs, and this feeling of disappointment overrode the pride he felt for all of his other accomplishments.

Making the three girls Ms. Lovel's responsibility had been the right decision. Now, perhaps things would work out for the FIGs and for Wood Rose. At least he could be comfortable with their future plans, because it was with his assistance all three girls had been accepted into excellent schools of higher learning once they left Wood Rose.

Just then there was a light knock on the door, and Jimmy Bob Doake whose shift didn't end for another hour poked his head in. "Is everything all right in here, Dr. Harcourt? Mrs. Ball thought there might be a problem."

"Everything is just fine, Jimmy Bob." Dr. Harcourt smiled, one of the few times Jimmy Bob had ever seen him do it. "Just fine."

* * *

After leaving Dr. Harcourt's office, Carolina stopped by the dormitory to leave a message for the FIGs with the dorm mother, Ms. Larkins. She had crossed the biggest hurdle by getting Dr. Harcourt's approval. She knew the expenses involved would be the stumbling block, which is why she offered to pay their way. After all, she had $50,000 sitting in a bank. She would use some of that. Now she would have to see how the FIGs felt about her plan. She hoped they would be thrilled, but until she discussed it with them, she had no way of knowing. If they didn't like her plan, life would be difficult at the very least.

Carolina found Ms. Larkins in the laundry room folding sheets.

"I just don't know when they could have done it," she bawled as soon as she saw Carolina. She flung herself and a wadded-up sheet still warm from the dryer at Carolina and whispered in her ear, "If you ask me, graduation for those three won't get here soon enough—if you know what I mean."

"No one is blaming you, Ms. Larkins. Everyone knows how well you look after all of the girls. It can't be easy."

Ms. Larkins grabbed another sheet from the dryer and thwacked it in the air, determined to remove any stubborn wrinkles or creases that didn't belong.

"When the FIGs get back from Sunday services, would you please tell them to come to my bungalow?"

Ms. Larkins nodded, sniffed, and thwacked the sheet again, this time causing it to snap loudly.

Back outside Carolina breathed in deeply. The thick greenish-yellow tree pollen had finally disappeared, replaced by the fresh woodsy scent of pine. Exhilarated, she jogged toward her bungalow. She hadn't told Dr. Harcourt about her personal reasons for getting involved with the Voynich Manuscript. Until now, she had only told Larry about her past, and he had been tremendously supportive and helpful in getting information—especially where it concerned her birth certificate. But she would tell the FIGs. Being totally honest and forthright with them was one reason why they respected her so much. She expected and received the same from them. She would show the FIGs what she had discovered so far to help them understand.

Outside her bungalow, she picked one of the hydrangea blooms, a delicate periwinkle blue with a tint of deep purple, which was just starting to open. It would look pretty in the orange carnival glass vase—a flea market find—in the middle of her kitchen table.

After putting the flower in water, Carolina went to her bedroom and pulled out the brown leather suitcase from under her bed that contained years of research. Her special project. It had been a while since she had looked at it, but it didn't matter. She knew every scrap of paper by heart.

Chapter Six

*L*yuba filled her basket with small bags of dried herbs, jars of ointment, and pretty bottles of oil. She also wrapped her crystal in a soft, black cloth and tucked it in at one end along with her Tarot cards, which she protected with a black silk scarf. She preferred to read palms—handwalking, she called it—but if someone asked for the crystal or cards, she was prepared. The last thing she added was the *parik-til* she had made, just in case.

It was getting on toward mid-morning—time for the villagers to be up and about. Most of the gypsy women had left earlier, preferring to ride in the back of the pickup truck. She set out walking on the road she remembered from before, feeling a mixture of dread and anticipation. Two other gypsy women, also walking into the village, hurried to join her.

"So, Lyuba, do you think we will have a good day?" The young woman who asked the question was eager, but untrained. She had much to learn about the ways of the settlers she wished to sell to. If she presented herself in an aggressive manner, they would turn away from her. Lyuba nodded but didn't speak. The other woman sensed Lyuba's mood and pulled the young woman back. It was better to leave Lyuba alone with her thoughts.

It had been a beautiful spring day, much like this one, when Lyuba decided to take her young daughter with her into the village. She was such a pretty, happy little girl—fair complexioned, large green eyes, and beautiful dark hair. Nothing like her parents who were dark skinned and showed all of the physical characteristics of the black tribe. It happened, a white child born into the black tribe, but only rarely. How proud Lyuba was of Carolina, a rare child who had been born with the gift. Normally, Lyuba would leave her daughter behind at the camp where she would be protected. She wasn't old enough to understand the ways of the settlers, or how to deal with them. But it was such a nice day. The little girl, not yet four years old, would draw attention. People would buy Lyuba's potions when they saw Carolina.

But that's not what happened. Lyuba knew

as soon as she got to the village that she had made a mistake in bringing her child. Evil was lurking nearby; all of the omens were present. She fled, taking the back streets out of town and then cutting through the gardens of the Old Villa. But the rushed pace tired her child, and carrying her slowed Lyuba. Instead of getting her daughter to safety, Carolina was taken by a man with the government agency. For weeks Lyuba begged him to give her back; after all, she was recently widowed, and Carolina was all she had left. In desperation, she even broke into the building where Carolina was kept in an attempt to find her only child. They could have had her arrested, but they did not. Nor would they relent. And then Lyuba knew. Because her powers were innate, bred through a bloodline of generations of psychics, she knew that Carolina was no longer there. They had given her away to other parents in another country.

Heartbroken, Lyuba did something she had never done before: She cursed the man who was responsible for her pain. She wanted to make him suffer as he had made her suffer. A short time later, the travelers broke camp and continued on their journey, never to return to the place that caused their tribe so much sadness—until now.

* * *

"Well, that was weird." Dara stepped out of the administrative building and into the bright sunshine, followed by Mackenzie and Jennifer. Several faculty members were watching two men rake the discarded limbs and leaves from the base of the now-denuded bush. When they saw the three girls, everyone casually turned and walked away in different directions, except for the two men who were doing the raking. "He didn't even punish us." Jennifer flipped her ponytail back and forth, something she usually did whenever she felt a keen sense of accomplishment.

"Not yet," said Mackenzie, her hazel eyes starting to show concern.

"He's not going to punish us," said Dara.

"What do you think he meant when he said Carolina will explain things. What things?" Mackenzie glanced around to make sure no one was close enough to overhear. "You don't think he fired her, do you?" The concern had now become worry.

All three girls stopped walking and stared at each other. "Come on," said Dara, pulling the other two in the direction of the cafeteria. "He told us to go to breakfast and then services, so we'd better do it.

Then we'll find Carolina."

* * *

Ms. Larkins was determined to do whatever necessary to avoid being sucked into the blame for what the FIGs had done. She alone was responsible for the girls' safe keeping between the hours of ten o'clock in the evening and seven o'clock in the morning. Other than severe illness or some natural disaster like a hurricane, there was no excuse for any of the girls to be out of bed, and certainly not out of their rooms, during those hours.

After the last offense, when the FIGs had foiled Dr. Harcourt's office, Ms. Larkins had taken added precautions to insure she would be awakened if anyone attempted to leave the dormitory in the middle of the night. It was a crude idea, a string tied from the outer door to a bell she had next to her bed, and it should have worked. It didn't. And now this. If Carolina wanted them to come to her bungalow after Sunday services, then, by gosh, she would make sure they got the message. With the sheet now partially folded, she positioned herself just outside the dormitory entrance, where she had full view of the administrative building. Within a few short minutes, the three girls appeared.

"Yoohoo," she called, waving the sheet, and in a matter of seconds she had delivered the message, generating even more anxiety in the highly-intellectual minds of the three FIGs.

* * *

Within the walls of Wood Rose, as with most closed communities, information could be sent and received through osmosis. Everyone knew everything that was happening, especially whenever there was a situation on campus. This morning, in the cafeteria, was no different, and all of the Wood Rose student-residents, seated at their assigned tables according to class in the dining room, were discussing what had taken place while they slept, and guessing what would come of it.

"Dr. Harcourt has to get rid of them," said Katherine, one of the graduating high school seniors who had thrived in the strict environment of Wood Rose and would continue her advanced studies in religion. "They are weird, and all they do is cause trouble."

Another girl—sophomore Lynda spelled with a "y" Corgill—who had entered Wood Rose a couple of years after Dara and Mackenzie, secretly admired the FIGs and didn't wish to see them punished. She also wished she had the nerve to do some of the things they did—sometimes. But still ...

"But what is it?" asked one of the 10-year-old middle-grade girls who had noticed the neatly pruned cylinder shape earlier that morning. The older girls standing nearby giggled.

The youngest Wood Rose girls, ages five through nine, sat together at one long table in the center of the dining room. They didn't know what was going on; only that something terrible must have happened, since all of the big girls were whispering. Usually, the older girls didn't whisper so much.

Separated from the long tables where the girls ate, at smaller, individual tables positioned in front of the floor-to-ceiling windows, which provided scenic views of the beautifully landscaped lawn, the faculty ate in intimate groups of two, three, or four, their conversations kept to low, hushed tones.

"What do you think they used for a model?" Even though the others at the table were thinking it, Dr. Rankin, the head of the biology department, boldly blurted out this question first. The other three faculty members seated at the table, all teachers at the elementary school level, only shook their heads.

At a table across the way in front of another window the conversation took on a different twist. "Maybe the FIGs didn't do it; maybe it is like one of those crop circles." Clyde Benson, the head of the physical education department, laughed out loud at this suggestion and then quickly sobered so as not to insult his colleague, the pretty Dr. Catherine Sullivan, head of the history department, whom he had been seeing with some regularity in their off hours.

As soon as Dara, Mackenzie, and Jennifer walked into the dining room, everything became quiet. Not even a dish rattled. The FIGs were accustomed to being made the prime subjects of gossip and chose to ignore it. They got their plates, filled them with food, and picked out one of the tables normally reserved for faculty, apart from everyone else, where they could talk without being overheard.

"Look," said Dara, scooping up some scrambled eggs onto her fork and cramming them into her mouth. "He wouldn't dare fire Carolina. For one thing, she hasn't done anything wrong. And another thing, who else would even want to teach us?"

"Yeah, but what if he holds her responsible?" asked Mackenzie, all of her problem-solving abilities suddenly consumed by concern and her lisp quite noticeable. She looked at Jennifer who was creating a picture by scattering the food around on her plate with a fork. "Are you going to eat that toast?" Mackenzie always ate more whenever something was bothering her.

Jennifer forked over her toast to Mackenzie, too worried to eat. The last thing she wanted was for Carolina to lose her job over something silly she and the other FIGs had done.

"I'll tell you what," said Dara, her dark eyes flashing, "If Thurgood fires Carolina, we will chop down his *Photinia fraseri, Peni erecti,* and be damned with it. After all, if it weren't for Carolina, we would have run away a long time ago."

Mackenzie and Jennifer nodded in silent agreement. They would fight this to the bitter end.

As soon as the FIGs left the cafeteria, new, more energized discussions erupted among students and faculty alike, amplifying the noise level around the large room by several decimals amidst the normal clatter of dishes and silverware being washed in the kitchen.

This went unnoticed, however, by the three females of intellectual genius; for after leaving the cafeteria, they hurried across the lawn to another single-story stone building. There they entered the

ornate doors of Alcott Chapel, walked past the two
large portraits painted in oils and the crystal vase
of fresh pink roses, and sat next to each other in
the front pew, alone, pensive, and consumed with
anxiety-produced repentance 20 minutes before
services were to commence.

* * *

Carolina placed the notebooks, which held
her hand-written notes and materials that included
a copy of the Voynich Manuscript itself, and the box
that contained the *parik-til* and her birth certificate
and other documents on the table centered in front
of the sofa. Then she brought the photograph, which
she kept displayed in a silver frame on her chest of
drawers, from her bedroom and placed it on the
table with the other things. She checked her watch.
It was a few minutes before 11. Services would be
ending shortly.

Carolina prepared her coffee maker for eight
cups, brought out the sugar bowl—for Mackenzie—
and filled the creamer—for Jennifer and Dara. Then
she fixed herself a piece of whole-wheat toast with a
little orange marmalade. She wasn't hungry, but she
knew she shouldn't drink coffee—especially black

coffee, the way she liked it—on an empty stomach. Everything was ready, and in a few minutes she heard a determined rap on the door. The FIGs had come.

Carolina opened the door and the three girls rushed in, all at once.

"We won't let him do it, Carolina," said Dara because she always spoke first.

"It just isn't fair," said Mackenzie, stumbling slightly over the contraction, "isn't."

Jennifer merely stood quietly just inside the door of Carolina's bungalow, tried to flip her ponytail, but her large blue eyes brimmed with tears instead.

"What are you talking about?" Carolina led the girls into the kitchen where she poured each one a cup of coffee. She handed the sugar bowl to Mackenzie, and the creamer first to Dara, and then to Jennifer, who was trying to wipe away her tears with one hand while balancing the coffee cup in the other. With their cups filled, and the desired amounts of sugar and cream added, Carolina led her guests into the living room and motioned for them to sit on the sofa.

Dara once again took the lead. "We won't let Thurgood fire you. If he does, we're out of here!"

"Fire me! No one is getting fired. In fact,

something really good has come out of this. But first ... you do know that you shouldn't have done that to Dr. Harcourt's bush, don't you?"

All three FIGs looked down in the vicinity of their feet. "Yes ma'am."

"It would be nice if each of you wrote him a note of apology."

All three girls jerked their heads up and stared at Carolina.

"Don't you?" she asked, this time with a little more emphasis.

"Okay," said Dara finally.

Carolina looked at Mackenzie and Jennifer. They both nodded.

"All right. Enough said on that subject." She knew they would be true to their word and follow through. "Now I want to talk about something else."

It was then that the girls noticed the notebooks on the table in front of them, the small wooden box, and the photograph.

"I want to tell you a story," began Carolina.

The story she knew so well was a fascinating one, wrapped in mystery, adventure, and romance. It was her priceless treasure. Now, as she told the story to them out loud, however, she wondered if it didn't sound a little ridiculous—like a young child's fantasy of finding a rare jewel. She needn't have worried. The FIGs were caught up in Carolina's special project from the moment she said the word *story*. And from that moment on, they would follow her to the ends of the earth.

Chapter Seven

*F*rascati, less than 10 kilometers south of Rome, was the nearest of the Castelli towns. As in times past, the gypsies camped on a hill nearby, once called Tusculum by the ancients, in the shadows of the Villa Mondragone, so named because of the many dragons carved into its brown stone edifice. The gypsies simply called it the Old Villa. Originally built on Roman ruins in the sixteenth century, it had survived through the centuries as home to various Catholic cardinals and periods of abandonment until, most recently, when it had been sold by the college of the Jesuits to the Second University of Rome. From their camp, it was an easy walk into Frascati, a rural village not yet marred by tourism. The villagers still held on to some of the old beliefs, making it easier for the gypsies to sell their wares. But even in Frascati, there was the foul scent of change. Lyuba noticed it; the others who had been there before did as well. Soon it would become a destination for tourists, with its fancy wine and its historical villa.

Lyuba strolled the streets, remembering the familiar and noting the unfamiliar. The building that housed the many government offices was still there. She reached into the folds of her skirt to feel for her lucky charm, the stone that she always carried with her. It comforted her. Unseen, she stood quietly in the shade of a large red maple tree, little more than a sapling all those many years ago, and remembered. Just when she thought she could no longer bear the pain and must leave, two women came out of the ornate door, talking and laughing. They were probably going somewhere to eat lunch. Lyuba stepped from the shade into the sunlight.

"Would the pretty lady like to have her fortune told?" she asked the younger of the two. The young ones usually liked to have their fortunes told. Both women stopped, and it was then that Lyuba recognized the older woman. Stunned, she couldn't say anything. Instead, she reached into her basket and pulled out the small pouch she had brought with her. "Keep this with you, and you will have many blessings," she said, handing it to the older woman.

She didn't wait to get paid; she simply left. For a moment, the two women wondered if they had even seen the gypsy, but they knew they had because Senora De Rossa held the *parik-til* the gypsy woman had given her.

"How strange," said the younger woman. "What do you suppose that was all about?"

The older woman remained quiet, staring into the shadows where the gypsy had been.

Lyuba hadn't been prepared to see her so soon, but she quickly recovered. After all, it was the reason she had returned to that place. She hadn't even known if the woman would still be there and, strangely enough, it gave her a feeling of happiness to know that she was. It was a good omen that she had brought the special *parik-til* she had prepared for her—the kind one who had tried to help her all those many years ago.

Lyuba returned to camp just before dusk, when the last of the sun's rays—the crown of thorns as she called it—were the only visible objects on the western horizon. The basket on her arm was empty except for the crystal wrapped in a soft black cloth and her Tarot cards. She had done well, but she always did. Maybe the Bandoleer had been right; it was time to face the negative forces from the past, and then move on.

* * *

The FIGs were familiar with part of the story—
that part where Carolina was taken from a foster
home when she was three years old and adopted by a
family named Branson. She had revealed that much
to them on one of their outings off campus.

"I had just turned 18 when they told me I was
adopted," Carolina said.

"That must have been hard," said Mackenzie,
who didn't know what it was like to have parents,
real or otherwise.

"Not really. You see, I had always suspected
something wasn't quite right. The peculiar way
people looked at me when I was introduced as
Carolina Branson; I looked nothing like my adoptive
parents. I don't look anything like my real parents
either, as far as that goes, but I just never felt totally
comfortable around my adoptive parents, at least
not in the way my friends did with their parents. It
was almost a relief when they told me. It somehow
all made sense then." She sipped her coffee and
picked up the wooden box on the table. "Anyway,
a few weeks before I started college, they gave me

this box. It contained my birth certificate and some other documents having to do with the adoption, a photograph of a man and woman whom I assume are my birth parents, and some money—things my birth parents had wanted me to have."

"Wow," said Dara. "Your birth parents must have really loved you."

Carolina smiled at the FIGs, knowing each of them had buried deep within them their own dreams and fantasies of what their parents were like had they known them, or, in Jennifer's case, if they had lived. She did the same thing. It was a coping mechanism when you were alone in the world; it helped make something wrong, right. "Naturally I cherished these things because my real parents wanted me to have them. But then, a short time later, just a week before I was to attend orientation at the university, I stumbled across something that has completely changed my life."

By this time all three girls were sitting on the edge of the sofa.

"Before starting my freshman year, my academic advisor had given me a list of books to read over the summer. On that list was a book about the Voynich Manuscript that also had several photographs of some of the actual manuscript pages."

"Wait a minute," said Jennifer. "What's the Voynich Manuscript?"

"The Voynich Manuscript is the most mysterious of all the texts in the world," answered Carolina.

"Didn't some top military code-breakers try to decipher it during World War II, but failed?" asked Dara.

"Yeah, and then some professor at the University of Pennsylvania went insane trying to figure it out," added Mackenzie.

"So why haven't I heard of it?"

"A lot of people have never heard of the Voynich Manuscript." Carolina opened one of her notebooks on the table and pulled out a sheaf of papers. "This is a copy of it." She handed it to Jennifer. "The original is seven by 10 inches, about 235 pages long, and it's made of soft, light-brown vellum. Small, but thick."

"Where is the original?" asked Jennifer.

"Now it is in the Beinecke Library at Yale University. A rare book expert in New York, named H.P. Kraus, donated it when he couldn't find a buyer for it. Before that, in 1912, a book collector by the name of Wilfrid M. Voynich discovered the manuscript in a chest with some other ancient manuscripts kept in the Jesuit College at the Villa Mondragone in Frascati, near Rome."

Carolina had the girls' full attention. "There was a piece of paper attached to the Voynich Manuscript when Wilfrid Voynich found it, which revealed that the manuscript was once part of the private library of Petrus Beckx S.J., 22nd general of the Society of Jesus. There are a lot of theories about its origins. Other notable people that may have been involved with the manuscript include Rudolph II, emperor of the Holy Roman Empire in the mid-1500s and early 1600s, Athanasius Kircher in the 1600s, who was considered one of the most learned men of his day, and Roger Bacon in the 1200s, who was a Franciscan friar."

Jennifer had moved onto the floor with several sheets of the manuscript spread out in front of her. "There are a lot of drawings," she commented, immediately drawn to the artwork in colors of red, blue, brown, yellow, and green, since one of her specialties was art.

"The contents of the manuscript appear to be divided into five categories. What you are looking at, Jennifer, is called the botanical section—plant drawings. There is also the astrological or astronomical section, the biological section, the pharmaceutical section, and then the last section, which is 23 pages of text arranged in short paragraphs, each beginning with a star. The last page in this section appears to be a Key of some sort."

Dara and Mackenzie picked out more pages of the manuscript and joined Jennifer on the floor.

"There seem to be word repetitions, like a code," said Mackenzie, who specialized in computers, math, calculus, and problem-solving.

"Maybe even two different languages," added Dara, whose knowledge of foreign languages included the ancient language of Sanskrit.

Not surprising, the girls had immediately picked up on some of the crucial findings about the manuscript. "No one knows what it means. It is written from left to right, and the lines scan from the top of the page to the bottom. The style is a flowing cursive script in an alphabet that has never been seen elsewhere ..." Carolina hesitated. "... until now."

Engrossed in the manuscript pages spread out before them and comfortable in their surroundings of brightly-colored, hand-sewn cushions, slip covers, and draperies, Carolina's admission first went unnoticed by the FIGs. Then everything became still. Dara was the first to grasp the meaning of Carolina's words—or maybe it was the tone of her voice that she picked up on.

"What do you mean, Carolina?"

Carolina removed an old, creased single sheet of paper, yellowed with age, which was now carefully protected in clear, acid-free paper. She handed it to Dara. "This was folded up in a *parik-til*, in the box with my birth certificate."

"A *parik-til*?" asked Jennifer.

"It is a small pouch filled with things to bring good luck or blessings." She held up the cloth bag and opened it for the girls to see. "Gypsies use them, but so do Native Americans as well as people from Central and South America and other parts of the world. When I got it, I had no idea what it was or what it meant. I knew the folded piece of paper was old and somehow important to me, since my birth parents included it with the other things they wanted me to have." Carolina stood up and walked over to the window. How well she remembered the overwhelming emotions she felt when she first saw those pages of the Voynich Manuscript in the book she was reading, and the realization that the ancient script was the same as that on the piece of paper, which had been preserved in her *parik-til*. "Anyway, as soon as I saw the photographs of some of the manuscript pages in the book I was reading, I made the connection. It was the same script as what was on this sheet of paper that I had been given."

All three FIGs crowded closely together to look at Carolina's treasure.

"Even more amazing is the fact that, according to my birth certificate, I was born in Frascati, Italy, the same place where the Voynich Manuscript was originally discovered."

For the next several minutes, only the hypnotic ticking of the clock hanging on the wall between the kitchen and living room could be heard while each girl studied Carolina's single page, wrapped in acid-free paper. Then everyone started talking at once.

The FIGs spent the rest of the day at Carolina's bungalow going over the material Carolina had amassed in her years of research, taking only a brief cafeteria break for lunch and dinner. When the clock struck nine o'clock that evening, Carolina made them return to their rooms in the dormitory so they would be there when lights went out at 10. They would start fresh the next morning and make their plans.

Chapter Eight

The young gypsy child called Bakro ran sobbing to his mother. "Milosh put a curse on me." His mother knelt down and enfolded him into her arms.

"Milosh doesn't have the power." She spoke quietly and in a voice she knew would comfort. "He is only playing games." She glanced across the dirt path that had once been part of the beautiful gardens of the Old Villa toward the small trailer where the Bandoleer stayed with his wife and boy. She was angry, but she would not let her young son know. Instead, she would settle it with the Bandoleer's wife. She had been much too lax with Milosh. He was getting out of hand and causing fear and bad feelings amongst the younger children. Pretending to put bad curses on them, and for what? Just to frighten! He needed to be punished.

She took her young son by the hand and led him into their hut. "It is time for bed, Bakro. Wash yourself, and then I will tell you a story."

The young child did as he was told, for he had no desire to disobey—not like Milosh.

* * *

Jimmy Bob Doake heard a light knock on his office door. It was probably one of the hair-brained, ego maniac teachers wanting something. None of them seemed able to get things done during regular hours. It was always after hours when they needed something, usually when he was watching one of his favorite teams on television, or writing one of his poems. It was Ms. Lovel.

"Hi, Jimmy Bob. I know it is late, but would you mind letting me into the machine room? I need to make some copies." In her arms she held a large file of papers.

"I don't mind one bit, Ms. Lovel." Unlike the others who taught at Wood Rose, Jimmy Bob liked Ms. Lovel. She was one of the few faculty members who didn't carry a chip on her shoulder. She always spoke to him when she saw him around campus and usually asked about his writing if she wasn't in a hurry. Once, when he was trying to find a word to rhyme with strange, she gave him a helpful little book that explained not all poetry had to rhyme or even be in meter. There was something called free verse, a flowing type of poetry that apparently had no rules. He had learned a lot from the little book. Since reading it, the volume of poems he produced had almost tripled.

He unlocked the room where various duplicating equipment and copy machines were kept, and then dutifully stood guard outside the door to give Ms. Lovel privacy and to make sure no harm came to her. Once she had finished, he locked up everything and then escorted Ms. Lovel back to her bungalow. After all, it was late and it was dark. And it was his responsibility to make sure no harm came to any of the residents of Wood Rose.

Back in her bungalow, Carolina went over the list of things she and the FIGs had discussed. There was so much to do. But now, at least, each of them would have a copy of the Voynich Manuscript and her own page so they could study them. The most pressing issue was the passports. Carolina's was up-to-date, as was Jennifer's. Dara and Mackenzie, however, didn't have passports. She checked her watch. It was after eleven o'clock, but he usually kept late hours anyway. And even if he was already in bed, he probably wouldn't mind. She picked up the phone and dialed long distance to Chapel Hill.

"Larry, I hope I didn't wake you."

"Are you kidding? You know me better than that. What's up, Carolina? I was starting to worry about you. I haven't heard from you in two days."

Carolina had first met Larry Gitani in the beginning of her freshman year at the university. Though an extremely private person, he was the most connected human being she had ever known. No matter what came up, he knew someone who could take care of it. He didn't talk much about his family, except to say his father was a widower, and he was from Italy. And sensing that he didn't want to talk about them, Carolina didn't ask questions.

They attended many of the same classes and both went on to graduate school. She studied foreign languages and psychology; he studied international law. There were many days and nights together, bent over books and research notes, sharing a pot of hot black coffee parked within easy reach, and simply being together. He became her best friend. They also spent hours exploring Carolina's adoption. Larry helped Carolina search for information about the region where she had been born, and her birth parents, he discovered, were gypsies.

When Larry got his doctorate, he elected to stay at the university and teach, which Carolina had also planned to do until the job offer came up at Wood Rose. It was Carolina's decision to leave the university that put a check on their relationship and where it was leading. That and Carolina's overwhelming need to learn the truth about her birth; for without that, she knew she could not succeed in any relationship, especially one that involved love and intimacy. Although they didn't see one another as often now, they still talked almost every day. The 30-mile distance between them hadn't changed her feelings for him or the fact that Larry would do anything in the world for her.

"Do you know anyone in the passport office?" Carolina asked. "I need two passports as soon as I can get them. Is that even possible?"

"Are these fake passports, or legit?" he asked.

Carolina giggled. "They are for two of my students. I am planning to take them and one other student to Italy for a mini study course, but our time is limited. We need to leave as soon as we can."

"I assume you are talking about the FIGs." Of course he was all too familiar with Carolina's three students and their expressions of creativity. "No problem." He told Carolina what he would need. "Does this mean you will be going to Frascati?"

"Yes."

Larry was well aware of Carolina's interest in Frascati, since she had shown him the contents of the wooden box. This was a big step for her—to finally go to the place of her birth. "Are you going to be all right? I mean, do you know what you want to accomplish?" Ever the pragmatist, Larry's concern was as logical as it was touching. "I assume this means you have told the FIGs about everything."

Carolina explained about the *Photinia fraseri* and her decision to make the trip now, taking the FIGs with her.

"I guess you showed them your special paper?" That was what he called the paper with the strange script.

"I did. And they immediately drew the same conclusions you and I did. We plan to go to the Villa Mondragone and do some research in the library there, assuming we will be allowed to. I hope to meet Senora De Rosa while we are there as well."

"I am happy for you, Carolina. Stay in touch, all right?"

"Thanks, Larry. I will. This means more to me

than you know."

Larry did know; he also knew that whatever she found at Frascati would have an impact on their relationship. Good or bad, he didn't know. "Well, you can pay me back by having dinner with me when you return so we can catch up."

He was right. They would need to catch up. He had always been there for her, patiently waiting; but she knew that couldn't continue indefinitely. He wanted a commitment from her and she—consumed with trying to find out who she was—had been both unwilling and unable. Maybe, once she returned, she could move forward with her life. Maybe, if it wasn't too late, she would finally make that commitment.

Later that night as she lay in bed, Carolina played the game once again: the psychic conflict between wanting primal familiarity or the search for novel experience. Familiarity was knowing and, more important, accepting who she was and her situation without question. The search for novel experience— her past, however, meant uncertainty, change, leaving the bounds of familiarity for something unknown. One was safe; the other, frightening. Yet, in the end, she knew what she must do. She had no choice. The decision had been made for her when she first learned she was adopted. She wanted to learn the truth. Without that, she would never feel complete as a person.

Sharing everything with the FIGs confirmed she was doing the right thing to explore her past. From the moment she first made the connection between her page and the pages of the Voynich Manuscript, she had felt an immense responsibility, even a sense of obligation, to discover the meaning of it all—even beyond learning her own background. She might not ever learn what any of it meant or her connection with it, but she had to try. And by involving the FIGs, she had at the very least given them something they would treasure for the rest of their lives. Hopefully, when it was all behind them, regardless of the outcome, that alone would somehow allow her to move on with her life, as well as help the FIGs look forward to the many wonderful possibilities in their own futures.

* * *

Dara's thoughts turned toward the mental exercise as she always did whenever she was familiarizing herself with a new language. It was her private world, her private language; it was how her mind functioned. It was what made her a genius.

First she established the root of each main word, or symbol in some cases, and assigned it a certain weight, or number. By knowing this, she could then figure out the origin of the word; from that, it was just a short step to recognizing its meaning. It was her own system, something she had taught herself as a child; but it worked, whether she was learning a new alphabet, the characters from an obsolete Chinese dialect, or hieroglyphics.

Next, she visualized the symbols or words she had noticed were most often repeated in the Voynich Manuscript. She thought of the manuscript's peculiarities, and then, turning away from the normal or obvious, she tried to think about what was abnormal and missing. The entire process was exciting to her; but even more exciting than working on translating the Voynich Manuscript was thinking about going to Italy with Mackenzie, Jennifer, and Carolina. Aside from leaving Virginia to live at Wood Rose, Dara had never been anywhere.

A late baby, Dara's seven older brothers and sisters had left home by the time she was born, so there was only her and her mama. Her first memories were those of always feeling hungry and the pungent odor of swamp mud. They had a small garden, she remembered, but nothing much ever came of it; and there was an old, smoke-blackened pot sitting out front in the yard that her mama burned kerosene in to keep the snakes away. Dara was smart, though, and she learned how to survive at a young age. Home was a rusted-out trailer set back in a thicket near a ditch bank that usually flooded whenever it rained. Years later, Dara no longer recalled what the inside of the trailer looked like. She only remembered sitting on the outside stoop with her mama, listening to tree frogs and cicadas while muddy flood waters lapped at their feet.

Property belonging to the United States Navy was just across the ditch bank, protected by a chain-link fence to keep out anyone who didn't belong. What she remembered about her mama was her beautiful, red painted mouth. She never knew her father, probably because her mother didn't know who her father was. That didn't mean Dara didn't know any men; her mama had many male friends that showed up late at night, dressed in their nice starched uniforms.

Most of the men wouldn't talk to her. But if they did, she would ask them to teach her new words. After all, they had traveled to foreign places, and Dara knew just enough to understand that people in other places spoke different languages. Sometimes the words they taught her weren't nice words, and they would laugh at her when she repeated them. Or sometimes they made up words just to get her out of the way. But it didn't matter. She played her game with the words, thinking about the heavy parts of the biggest words, giving them a number, and figuring out where they came from.

Neighbors just as poor as Dara and her mama would occasionally give them food or clothes. And sometimes, when one of the men left a little money, Dara's mama would take her into town to buy a piece of nickel candy at the store. That's what happened the last time Dara saw her mama. "You wait here, pretty girl," her mama had told her, poking her finger into one of the sausage curls on Dara's head to smooth it out. Dara waited hours for her mama to come back for her. But she never did.

When social services stepped in, Dara was given clean clothes to wear and food to eat. She was also given a battery of tests, called psychological and educational performance evaluation tests, to determine where she should be placed in school. Astonishingly, she ranked off the charts. Thinking a scoring error occurred, the child psychologist administering the tests gave them to Dara again, along with several different tests. The second time

Dara scored even higher, especially in the area of verbal skills—word recognition, association, and assimilation. The psychologist then consulted Dr. Doris James, the head of social services for the State of Virginia. She decided to send Dara to Wood Rose Orphanage and Academy for Young Women. Dr. Harcourt was a long-time friend, and she knew of the sterling reputation he had maintained at Wood Rose over the years. She felt confident that Dara Roux, a gifted child with an obvious proclivity toward foreign languages, would be given the attention and encouragement she needed. In return, the State of Virginia would pay Wood Rose for taking care of her.

* * *

All of her life Mackenzie had been afraid. The thought of not living up to someone else's expectations—it didn't matter whose—caused her to fear she wouldn't be adopted. So she focused on the things she enjoyed the most and caused the least amount of criticism. Even at a young age that focus was on numbers. She loved them—playing with them, seeing how many ways she could make them relate to each other in unusual ways, and relate to her. Because of her exceptional mathematical skills, at age seven she was transferred from an orphanage in upstate New York to Wood Rose Orphanage and Academy for Young Women. There, another seven-year-old child with exceptional abilities had also recently been admitted. It was at Wood Rose that Mackenzie broadened her focus to include calculus, algebra, algorithms, geometry, and numerical codes.

Dara Roux, Mackenzie soon learned, was the other gifted student, and the two became inseparable. Each girl sensed the other's needs as only one with brilliance could. And when the two girls turned nine years old, the age when the possibility for adoption drops by 85 percent, Mackenzie's old fear of failure was replaced with a new fear: not fitting in with the other girls at Wood Rose who also had not been chosen to live with a forever family. Dara wasn't afraid of anything, and when she learned of Mackenzie's new fear, she was quick to console her. "Who wants to be put in a family with all those rules?" reasoned Dara. "You wouldn't be able to do anything—not like we can do here."

Mackenzie silently calculated that being one kid out of 38 under the watchful eye of 10 Wood Rose faculty members and 25 members of the staff and administration didn't greatly increase the odds of her being able to do whatever she wanted. But, as the years passed, and with Dara as her best friend, her fear diminished, and her lisp only became pronounced in situations that caused extreme nervousness.

With the arrival of Jennifer, the strong union between Mackenzie and Dara was stretched to include this strange girl who was either poised for battle or locked in a silent world of musical notes. It had been only Dara and Mackenzie for so long. But even as different as Jennifer was, they could each relate to the other; she fit in. They shared a common goal: trying to survive in an environment where they were considered odd and different. Therefore, within a short time, Jennifer also became Mackenzie's friend.

When Carolina came to Wood Rose, for the first time in her life Mackenzie actually knew what happiness felt like. Unspoken dreams suddenly became possibilities under Carolina's tutelage, and she began to visualize her future filled with accomplishments and successes once she left Wood Rose. And now, all of this news about the Voynich Manuscript made the reality of a successful future closer than she ever dared to hope.

She sat up in bed and flipped on the flashlight she kept under her pillow. Then she reached for her calculator, which was never far away, and began methodically punching in figures. Even though everything about the manuscript seemed unrelated and disconnected, there was a certain mathematical logic to it. As Dara had pointed out, maybe it was two languages that had been combined.

* * *

A cadence had started beating in Jennifer's head the moment she saw the Voynich Manuscript. It was beating now as she lay in bed, in the darkness of her room. She wasn't sure what it meant; only, like before whenever a new musical composition stirred in her mind, it first came to her in a black and white image—like a charcoal drawing. Over time it would gradually change to color; and along with the color would come a beat—the cadence as she called it. First softly, then pronounced, loud, and vibrating. But it was only after the black and white image and then the colored image emerged, when she felt the vibration of the cadence, that she knew she needed to capture its musical essence. This was when she wrote the notes on eight-stave musical paper as she heard them in her mind. This time, as she wrote the notes, she knew it was part of the answer to deciphering the manuscript.

The emotional pain, she thought of it as a massive rock, that she had been carrying with her for as long as she could remember, even before her parents' death, had lessened—the rock had started to get smaller, since she had come to Wood Rose, especially with Carolina's arrival. In fact, even with all of the exciting events of the day, there was hardly any sign of it at all. Jennifer shifted slightly against her pillow as though to test it. It was still there, but it didn't hurt nearly as much.

Jennifer was a wild child. A musical prodigy from the age of two, she had kept her parents in a state of exhaustion with her sudden and unexplained emotional outbursts, which were followed by days of deep depression. After consulting a long line of pediatricians and being prescribed an equally long list of different drugs, Jennifer remained a child that could not and would not be controlled. Public schools were out of the question; she had to be taught by private tutoring.

By the time she reached puberty, she had composed a symphony for a full orchestra, a fugue that she had also transcribed into a rondo, numerous individual pieces that focused on two or three single instruments such as the piano, violin, and cello, and a piano sonata. It was the sonata that gained her world-wide prominence when she performed it at Carnegie Hall over Thanksgiving the year she turned 13. She had not performed again since then, at least not in public.

The temper tantrums and bouts with depression became less frequent for a while, and her parents began to travel to Europe. Sometimes they would take Jennifer. As long as she had her portfolio filled with blank, eight-stave paper with her so she could write down the music that filled her very being, then things might be all right. But not always. There were still problems and, often, embarrassing moments. Gradually, Jennifer's parents began leaving Jennifer behind with an assortment of hired help. They were escaping from her and her unpredictable behavior, and Jennifer knew it. They didn't know how to control her, any more than she knew how to control herself.

Ironically, the car accident occurred after returning from a trip to England. They had gone to the neighborhood grocery store for a few items. Both were killed instantly. There were no close relatives, at least none who were willing to take care of Jennifer. So with a little over a year to go before reaching adulthood, Jennifer was placed in the Wood Rose

Orphanage and Academy for Young Women. She was assured they had an excellent music department and art department, both nationally recognized, where she could continue her studies.

The excellent music and art departments, however, weren't prepared for Jennifer. At 16 years old, she possessed more talent than the six faculty members that comprised the two departments. It would have been a disaster if it hadn't been for Dara and Mackenzie. They understood what it was like to try to communicate on a level where others would understand, but not succeed. To want to be included, to want desperately to be like everyone else but knowing that was impossible, caused feelings of resentment—because they weren't.

Jennifer immediately fit in as a FIG. When her temper got out of control, Dara calmed her. When she needed space and solitude because the pictures filling her head had changed into so many notes that she couldn't write them down fast enough, Mackenzie understood and protected her. For a while, they just had each other. Then Carolina came. Instinctively they knew Carolina was one of them, and they loved her for it.

Now, in the quiet of her room, Jennifer concentrated on the colorful picture in her mind as it changed into a musical cadence. What was it saying? What was its meaning? It was beating out musical notes, and she began rapidly writing them down on eight-stave musical paper illuminated by a flashlight.

* * *

Senora De Rossa couldn't sleep. She couldn't stop thinking about the gypsy she had seen that day on her way to lunch. Even though it had been many years ago, she recognized her—the dark skin and high cheekbones, and those eyes, penetrating all that she saw, yet revealing nothing. She had always known that one day she would return.

Young and still impressionable, the senora had just started working at the records office all those years ago. Anthony Liruso was head of the department then, an outsider from the Calabria region, and he was determined to get rid of the gypsies in the area. "They are a nuisance, and they bring crime," he had told her. He had taken her with him on that particular day when he heard a gypsy was selling potions with a small child. He found them in the gardens of the Old Villa. She would never forget how the gypsy had screamed at him as he ripped the little girl from her arms. She pleaded with him to return the child to the gypsy. Even though the child didn't look like a gypsy, she felt that she really belonged to the gypsy woman. But he was determined. In just a short time, Liruso arranged for an American couple to adopt her.

The gypsy woman came one time after that, seeking her out, carrying a small wooden box that was to be given to the child when she reached the age of 18. Because the gypsy woman trusted her, Senora De Rossa had taken it, promising to somehow get it to her daughter. It was only days later when Liruso suddenly died. Heart attack, the coroner said. Some of her colleagues said it was because he wasn't from the Lazio region; he didn't know their ways. He had been brought up on thick tomato sauces instead of the lighter garlic sauces. The olive oil wasn't as good in the Calabria region; it had weakened his heart. But she knew better. She had heard the screams of the distraught gypsy mother; and she knew she had cursed him.

Eventually, after years of hard work and dedication to her job, Senora De Rossa became head of the records office. Soon after that she was contacted by a woman from America trying to get information on her birth and adoption. Senora De Rossa knew immediately who the young woman was, and more than anything she wanted to help her. She wanted to help her for the gypsy woman's sake. But the Italian laws forbade her from giving her what she asked. So instead, she gave her information about Italian adoptions in general, and about how and why the system worked against the gypsies. Each bit of information she gave to Carolina was a clue to Carolina's past.

Carolina was bright. It didn't take her long to make the correct assumptions. And now her mother—the gypsy woman—had returned. Senora De Rossa would call Carolina, this time giving her the background information of her birth name. She would do it because Liruso had made a mistake by taking the little girl from her mother. She would do it for the gypsy woman.

Chapter Nine

Lyuba was awakened by shouts coming from the Bandoleer's trailer. She covered herself with her robe and stepped out into the early morning light. It was Rupa, Bakro's mother.

"I will not have your son frightening Bakro. You need to punish Milosh. He has no compassion for others."

Djidjo, the Bandoleer's wife, placed her fists on her wide hips. "Maybe you make your son timid," she yelled into the face of the other woman. "You always wanted a daughter." This was a terrible insult, and the other gypsies who had been awakened by the arguing women watched in stunned silence.

Lyuba had watched the Bandoleer leave camp in the night—to where, she did not know. He needed to be here now and stop this nonsense before it got worse. It was not good for the morale of the tribe. Now, more than ever, they needed to be united.

Rupa spat on the ground in front of Djidjo, then turned and walked away. She had made her point, as had Djidjo. Nothing more needed to be said—until next time.

Milosh watched from the darkness of the trailer. He knew he had gotten away with it again—putting curses on the younger children. Only Bakro had told on him though. He would make Bakro pay. Quietly he slipped back into his bed and pretended to be asleep when his mother came in and stood over him. Her anger would cool and she would forget. But he would not; he would make Bakro regret telling his mother.

Lyuba went back inside her hut and began preparations for the day. She would work extra hard with Milosh when he and the other children came to learn. She needed to stop the evil that was filling his spirit before it was too late.

* * *

The FIGs were awake, showered, and dressed hours before the other residents. They spent that quiet time before breakfast in Dara's room going over the manuscript together and getting more familiar with its unusual construction: the so-called divisions.

"What we have here is the equivalent of 246 quarto pages, but there seem to be some pages missing," said Dara, her back pressed against the headboard of her bed. "Those might be what Carolina has."

Jennifer was sitting on the floor with her back against the wall, manuscript pages scattered around her. "There are 212 pages with text and drawings, 33 pages contain text only, and the last page contains what might be the Key."

"The way I see it, this is how the five categories of the manuscript are divided." Mackenzie's calculator, which applied logarithms and other difficult mathematical calculations and stored information much like a tiny computer, was attached to the waistband on her skirt. She detached it from her waist and punched several buttons. "The first and largest section—the botanical—contains 130 pages of plant drawings with accompanying text. The second, which is the astrological and astronomical section, contains 26 pages of drawings. The third section contains four pages of text and 28 drawings, which appear to be biological in nature. The fourth section contains 34 pages of drawings, which are pharmaceutical in nature. Finally, the last section contains 23 pages of text arranged in short paragraphs, each beginning with a star. This section is sometimes referred to as the recipes section, and might have been some sort of calendar or almanac. Page 24 of this section contains the Key only, which might have been a previous owner's attempt to decipher the thing." She put the calculator back in its holder. "I applied ELS—Equal Distance Letter Sequence Code—to the entire text, and nothing works out."

"Have you been able to tell anything about the language?" Jennifer asked Dara.

"For one thing, none of the Romance languages could be the base for the words in the text, but there is a certain syntax and language-specific word order similar to Sanskrit. Also, there is a repetitiousness of the text."

"Like a cadence," Jennifer said.

Dara nodded. "I also checked the entropy, which is a numerical measure of the randomness of text. The lower the entropy, the less random and the more repetitious it is. The entropy of what we have here is lower than that of most human languages; only some Polynesian languages are as low." She picked up several pages. "There are also some peculiarities worth noting: The text has very few apparent corrections; the structure of words is extremely rigid; and some characters in the key-like sequences don't appear anywhere else in the manuscript. Also, when I use Zipf's law of word frequencies, the text follows roughly the first and second characteristic of a natural language."

"And Zipf's law is what?" asked Jennifer.

"Originally, Zipf's law stated that in a corpus of natural language utterances, the frequency of any word is roughly inversely proportional to its rank in the frequency table. So, the most frequent word will occur approximately twice as often as the second most frequent word, which occurs twice as often as the fourth most frequent word, etc. The term now refers to any of a family of related power law probability distributions."

"If I didn't know any better, I would say someone wrote the same manuscript in several languages, cut them all up into pieces, threw them into the air, and then pieced them back together again, not caring which piece with what language landed where," said Mackenzie. "Anything special about the drawings, Jennifer?"

"Many of them are crudely drawn, and according to what I found on the Internet last night, many scientists feel that some of the drawings of plants and galaxies were invented."

"What if ..." Dara hesitated, thinking about what she wanted to say, "What if this is something that was written over 500 years ago by gypsies? After all, they were known to borrow whatever they needed to suit their purposes, including language. What if this was like their bible or book of life as they understood it, each section addressing particular issues, like medicine, religion, science, or astronomy." She looked at her two friends to see if they were following her. They were. "I mean, it would be nothing for them to create an entirely unique language unknown to man with pieces and bits taken from their own experiences as well as taken from other sources."

"What an idea," said Mackenzie.

"Which might explain why that page with the same script was with Carolina's birth certificate," continued Jennifer. "Carolina said her birth parents were gypsies."

"Which makes Carolina a gypsy, too," added Mackenzie.

"And that might explain why they wanted that page to be part of her inheritance," said Dara, completing the thought.

Just then the bell rang, indicating it was time to go to breakfast. They had already spent five hours working on the manuscript. They quickly put away the papers and headed for the cafeteria. Carolina had told them she wanted to take them into town after breakfast that morning to shop for suitable travel clothes. They had never felt happier.

* * *

Carolina had set her alarm for 5 A.M. She wanted to call Senora De Rossa who worked in the records office in the town of Frascati. There was a six-hour time difference, so by calling that early on Eastern Standard Time, she hoped to catch her before she went to lunch. She hoped the senora could suggest a place where she and the FIGs could stay.

Carolina met Senora De Rossa when she first started researching the information on her birth certificate. She had been surprised to learn there even was such an office, especially in a town with a population that numbered only 22,000, less than half the size of Chapel Hill. Being fluent in Italian, Carolina easily navigated the Italian version of red tape until she eventually wound up talking to Senora Lucia De Rossa. When Carolina explained that she was looking for information about her birth parents and her own birth and infancy, Senora De Rossa seemed to take a special interest. Carolina soon learned why. Hers was one of the first cases the senora had been involved in when she started working in the records office. They had talked several times since then, and each time Senora De Rossa had given Carolina additional information concerning her background.

"It is so good to hear from you, Carolina." Carolina smiled when she heard the familiar voice heavily flavored with an Italian accent. "I was going to call you today. I think I have some more information that might interest you."

Carolina immediately felt her adrenaline surge, which usually happened whenever she talked to Senora De Rossa, and grabbed the pad of paper and pen she always kept handy.

"The Lovel name is from an old and powerful English family. The gypsies who adopted it seem to have imagined that it had something to do with love for they translated it by *Camio* or *Caumio*, that which is lovely or amiable. *Camio* is connected with the Sanscrit *Cama*, which also signifies love, and is the appellation of the Hindoo god of love. If all tales be true, then those who are born by that divinity are black, which is perhaps why the gypsy tribe adopted it. The Lovel tribe is decidedly the darkest of all the Anglo-Egyptian families. They are generally called by the race the *Kaulo Camioes,* the Black Comelies.

"Now, this is where it gets interesting as far as you are concerned. There was a branch of Lovels that split from the original English tribe and settled in Italy, around the area of Frascati, where your birth certificate indicates you were born. I traced their origins as far back as the fourteenth century. There is a good possibility that they were around even before that, but instead of being known as gypsies back then, they were called land tramps. Does any of this make sense to you, Carolina?"

Carolina laughed. "Well, it makes sense, Senora De Rossa, except I am not black. I have dark hair, but my eyes are green, and I have a pale complexion with freckles."

The senora was prepared. "There might be an explanation for that." She put her mouth closer to the phone receiver and lowered her voice. "It is common knowledge that gypsies steal children— pretty children—usually in the community near where they are camped. But they also steal children from other gypsy tribes. This problem continues today. It is not widely known, but we have a special unit within our *guardia di financa* who do nothing but search the gypsy camps for children who obviously do not have gypsy characteristics, such as green or blue eyes and fair complexions."

"What happens to the children?" asked Carolina.

"They are removed and placed into State custody."

Carolina was astonished. How could the police assume, based on physical appearance alone, that the children had been stolen?

"There are several published reasons for the removal of these children, the most common being *sfruttamento di minori*."

"Exploitation of minors," Carolina translated.

"That is correct. If children are caught begging or selling knick-knacks either on their own or even in the presence of their parents, they are breaking the law. Truancy is another reason given. Most gypsy children are taught within the camps where they live. Their parents do not trust outsiders and, therefore, do not allow their children to attend public schools. Also, unsanitary conditions might be used as a reason to remove a child from its gypsy parents."

"What happens to these children once they are in State custody?"

"Once the child is in State custody, it is rarely returned to the gypsy family. It is usually put up for adoption." Senora De Rossa waited before continuing. "So, you see, Carolina, there are a number of things that might explain what happened to you. You might have been born into a gypsy family, but stolen by the black tribe, which would explain why you don't have the typical Lovel characteristics and features. Then, because you obviously didn't look like a member of the Lovel tribe, you were made a ward of the State and later adopted." The senora waited for Carolina to grasp what she was telling her. "Also, Carolina, there are those instances when a child such as yourself, with no gypsy physical characteristics, is born into the black tribe without any logical explanation. It just happens."

Everything that Senora De Ross was saying made sense. However, nothing about it explained how she came to be adopted in North Carolina rather than Italy, or why the document resembling the Voynich Manuscript was placed in the *parik-til* with her birth certificate. There had to be more to the mystery.

"Is there something else that worries you, Carolina?" Senora De Rossa had picked up on Carolina's hesitation.

"No, Senora De Rossa." She had revealed her own manuscript page to the FIGs, and, of course, to Larry, but she wasn't ready to tell anyone else. Not yet. "You have been very helpful, and I can't thank you enough." Then she told the senora the purpose of her call and of her plans to travel to Frascati with three of her students. They would stay for five weeks working on a research project, she explained.

"I know just the place where you can stay. It isn't a fancy hotel, but it is clean and comfortable. You will find it convenient as well. The proprietor is a good friend, a cousin actually. Both she and her husband speak a little English. I will check with her at lunch to make sure the apartment is available. If it is, I will call you back to give you all of the details."

* * *

Shopping with the FIGs took most of the day. They needed clothes and luggage. Jennifer had clothes and luggage, but not at Wood Rose. Everything had been stored away for her until she graduated from Wood Rose and decided to return to New York. They also stopped by a local photographer's to get passport photos made for Dara and Mackenzie. Then they drove to Chapel Hill with the photos and other information Larry had said he would need. He was in class, as Carolina knew he would be, but she left everything in his office where he would find it. By the time they got back to Wood Rose, it was the dinner hour.

Larry had told Carolina he could get the passports delivered to her by special courier late Wednesday. She called the airlines and made reservations for the four of them. They would fly to Rome, Italy, from Raleigh-Durham International on Thursday at noon, and had a short layover and change of planes at New York LaGuardia Airport. Meanwhile, the FIGs had all day Tuesday and Wednesday to finish their research paper on Mary Shelly's Frankenstein character, and to write their notes of apology to Dr. Harcourt. They each also had a copy of the manuscript along with a copy of Carolina's own page to work on independently.

While they were out shopping, Senora De Rossa had called back and left a message. The apartment was available and her cousin was holding it for Carolina and her students. Carolina wrote down the address and phone number of the proprietor along with the flight information to give to Mrs. Ball. Then she made a copy for herself and put it with her passport and other papers to take with her. As an afterthought, she looked inside her small wooden box and took out her *parik-til*. It wouldn't hurt to take it along as well. After all, it was supposed to keep her and her loved ones safe, as far as she knew. And that was what she wanted for herself and for her FIGs.

Chapter Ten

Milosh watched his mother leave with Lyuba and the other women to go into the village to sell their wares. Once he was sure she was gone, he pulled the large book of curses out of his father's trunk. Most of the curses required special herbs and other ingredients. Lyuba would have what he needed.

Outside, he walked around the campsite. Only a few, old travelers stayed behind to look after the young kids while their parents went into the village. When he was sure no one was looking, he slipped into Lyuba's hut. Everything was neat and in order. It had a nice smell, not like the musty smell of the trailer he and his parents lived in. There were several shelves behind a curtain on one of the far walls that held her herbs. He smiled when he found two of the ingredients he was looking for. He would use them

on Bakro for being such a baby. He carefully emptied
the herbs into the small paper sack he had brought
with him and stuffed it under his shirt where it
wouldn't be noticed.

Next to Lyuba's bed on a small table he noticed
a photograph of a young child. It was protected in a
silver frame that had a strand of red wool entwined
around the outer edge. Who was this child, he
wondered, picking it up to examine it more closely.
The young girl didn't look like she was from their
tribe. She had light skin, and her eyes were green.
With the photograph, pressed under the protective
glass, was a lock of hair that had been tied with the
same red wool that was on the frame. For as long as
he had known Lyuba, she had been alone. She didn't
even have a husband. So why did she have a picture
of this little girl? He took off the back of the frame
and removed some of the hair from its red binding.
Then he dropped it in his sack along with the herbs.
After replacing the back of the frame, he returned the
photograph to the table and, checking to make sure
no one was around, he quietly slipped out the door.

* * *

Senora De Rossa wasn't all that surprised

when Carolina told her of her plans to visit Frascati with three of her students. She had expected her to come eventually. How coincidental that the gypsy—Carolina's mother—had returned now as well. She examined the *parik-til* the gypsy had given her. The gypsy had told her to keep it close and she would receive many blessings. She would have to be very careful. If it were revealed that she had helped an adoptee locate her birth mother, she would lose her job. She thought back to the things she had told Carolina. It was mostly general information, but information that applied specifically to Carolina and her adoption. Also, there was the matter of the box. She had made up the story about an agreement between Carolina's birth parents and the agency to tell the Bransons to give the box to Carolina. No one else in the adoption office even knew about it. It was because of her that Carolina received it on her 18th birthday.

The senora rubbed the back of her neck. It had been wrong for Liruso to take the child the way he did. She believed it then and she believed it now. She only wanted to do what was right, and if that meant helping Carolina when she arrived, that's what she would do. Then, whatever happened, it was out of her hands.

Senora Del Rossa gently pressed the *parik-til* against her face—it had the sweet scent of roses and other herbs she didn't recognize—and then tucked it into her bra. She would be mindful of what the gypsy had told her and keep it close.

* * *

The passports were delivered to Carolina late Wednesday evening by special courier, just as Larry said they would be, under the watchful eye of Jimmy Bob Doake. After all, it was highly unusual for anything to be delivered by courier to the campus of Wood Rose, late or not. But Ms. Lovel seemed to be excited about receiving the package from the courier, so Jimmy Bob had to assume it was all right. Once Ms. Lovel signed for it, Jimmy Bob escorted the courier back to the main gate and waited until he was sure the guy wouldn't try to slip back in.

Jimmy Bob was proud of the fact that there had never been any problems of that sort during the entire 30 years he had been on watch, at least nothing serious. Once there was an incident with some squirrels making nests in the rafters of the dormitory. It had upset Ms. Larkins and the girls tremendously, all those strange scratching noises in the middle of the night. Fortunately, though, he had a cousin who was an exterminator, and with Jimmy Bob's assistance, the squirrels were humanely removed and everything returned to normal in a matter of days. Still, with all of the terrorists around these days, not to mention the plain old garden variety nut jobs, he just couldn't be too careful. He had heard that Ms. Lovel was taking her three students on a trip to Italy. Apparently it involved a special research project, and it was important that nothing disrupt her plans. At least that is what Dr. Harcourt had told him. He would certainly do his part to insure that nothing happened to prevent her and the FIGs from making the trip.

* * *

The trip itself wasn't perfect in every way, but close—at least in the minds of the four travelers from Wood Rose. The planes both in Raleigh-Durham and New York LaGuardia were on time, which was good. The weather was comfortable, which was also good. Carolina and her FIGs were also eager with anticipation of things to come, which wasn't all good. Even as a child, whenever Carolina got excited she had to go to the bathroom. Luckily she had an aisle seat, but it was a nuisance nonetheless.

The FIGs hadn't stopped talking since leaving Wood Rose.

"What if they lose our luggage?" asked Dara. Sitting next to the window, she watched the assortment of suitcases, boxes and other containers of different sizes and shapes leave the conveyor belt and disappear into the gaping darkness of the large cargo hold of the Delta plane.

"Then we'll buy what we need in Rome," answered Carolina, returning from a bathroom trip.

"What kind of car are we getting?" asked Jennifer as she flipped her ponytail.

"I asked for an automatic," said Carolina. "I'm not too good with a stick shift." Carolina stepped back into the aisle and headed for the lavatory.

"I can cook for us," offered Mackenzie when Carolina returned, "if there's a kitchen where we'll be staying."

Carolina squeezed back into her seat and nodded. Mackenzie had learned how to cook at Wood Rose and she enjoyed it.

"I wonder what the apartment will look like," said Dara.

And so it went.

The FIGs looked like completely different girls

wearing the jeans and t-shirts they had picked out for the trip. In honor of the occasion, and much to Carolina's relief, Jennifer had also decided to wear thong panties while away from Wood Rose—a small step up from wearing no underwear at all, but a step nonetheless. As the girls chattered, Carolina let her thoughts turn toward what she hoped they would accomplish during their five weeks abroad. For one thing, they wanted to spend some time in the library at the Villa Mondragone where the Voynich Manuscript had been discovered. It was a university now, but, nevertheless, it would at least give them a historical sense of the place.

Carolina was also looking forward to meeting Senora De Rossa. The senora was her one connection to her birth parents. Over the years, she had been a tremendous help, guiding her toward information and truth concerning her own adoption. But Carolina suspected she knew more than she had revealed. Perhaps it was out of fear of losing her job, for Carolina had researched the Italian laws regarding adoption and knew the senora had probably revealed more to her than she should have. But it might be something else as well, and maybe by meeting her in person, she would be more open and forthcoming with what she knew.

Carolina also had to allow for the possibility that maybe they wouldn't learn anything at all. She still wanted to at least try. And regardless of the outcome, once they returned to Raleigh she would contact the Beinecke Library at Yale University and let them know about her special paper. She had kept it a secret long enough.

Carolina reclined her seat and, listening to the giggles and continuous chatter of the FIGs in the background, fell into a peaceful sleep. Some hours later she was awakened by the need to visit the lavatory and an announcement that they were an hour outside of Rome. Breakfast was being served.

* * *

As far as the FIGs were concerned, their mission was two-pronged: Investigate the Voynich Manuscript and make their own conclusions concerning its meaning and origin; and, help Carolina find out as much as possible about her birth parents and the events leading to her adoption. After discussing it with Carolina, they had decided they needed to get a better handle on the history of ownership of the Voynich Manuscript—that would be their starting point. Dara pulled out some notes from her new shoulder bag, bought specifically for this trip and this purpose. Mackenzie unfolded a map she removed from her shoulder bag, which was identical to Dara's, and Jennifer took a pen and pad from her shoulder bag, to write down anything important. It matched the other two.

"This is what we know," said Dara. "The Voynich Manuscript enters recorded history when it surfaces at the court of Emperor Rudolf II of Bohemia in the mid 1500s. There is a letter written by a Prague doctor and scientist named Johannes Marci that states that Rudolf bought the manuscript for 600 ducats."

"He also wrote that he thought Roger Bacon was the manuscript's author," added Jennifer.

"Right," said Dara. "The next known owner is an alchemist named Georgius Barschius, who graduated from the Jesuit University in 1603. No one knows how he got the manuscript, but when he died in 1662, he left all of his alchemical collections and library, including the Voynich Manuscript, to his good friend, Marci.

"Marci tried to get the thing translated by the Jesuit Philosopher Athanasius Kircher, and apparently that is when it was added to the private library of the General of the Society of Jesus. The manuscript, along with the other valuable items in the library, disappeared until they showed up at the Villa Mondragone in Frascati in the late 1800s. Then, in 1912, when the Villa was trying to raise money for restorations, they sold the manuscript along with several others to W. Voynich.

"And now it is in the Rare Book and Manuscript Library at Yale University."

"I wonder if any of the other manuscripts that were with the Voynich had the same script?" said Jennifer.

"That's one thing we can check out—if they let us into the library. A lot of the books that Voynich bought were sold to the Vatican. But not all of them. And, of course, he only bought a fraction of what was at the Villa Mondragone. So that will be a good place for us to explore."

Mackenzie glanced over at Carolina to make sure she was asleep. "I have compared Carolina's page with every page we have of the manuscript, and it doesn't seem to belong to any of the sections."

Dara nodded. "I know. It looks like the same script, but yet it doesn't quite fit in with any of the Voynich sections."

"Maybe hers is from a different manuscript altogether," suggested Jennifer.

"Or maybe it is complete just as it is." Dara looked at her two friends. She had spent the past several days thinking of nothing but the manuscript. She held with her original thought that it was written in more than one language—or perhaps dialects—based on counts of character pairs and words. Jennifer had pointed out that there appeared to be two or more different handwriting styles as well, at least in the Voynich. Carolina's page was a separate style altogether, which indicated it was from a different source.

Jennifer began to write musical notes on the eight-stave paper she had brought with her. "Maybe if we can find out more about Carolina's box, which had everything in it, that will help us find out more about her parents. Carolina said Senora De Rossa sent it to her when she turned 18, so she must have gotten it from Carolina's birth parents."

"I also want to learn more about the gypsy language," said Dara. "From what I have been able to determine, it has a definite connection to Sanskrit."

Mackenzie nodded in agreement. "All we can do is try."

Each of the FIGs sat back in her seat thinking of what was ahead of them. In a way, each of them was seeking out their own truth, and, just like

Carolina, it was the most exciting thing that had ever happened to them.

* * *

Once they landed and retrieved their luggage, Carolina located the car rental desk. There was a slight mix-up in that she was given a stick shift rather than the automatic she had reserved. However, they soon straightened out the mistake and left Fiumicino airport, following the signs for *ROMA*. Twenty minutes later they were in downtown Rome and in more traffic congestion than Carolina had ever seen in her entire life.

"There's the Coliseum," squealed Mackenzie from the back seat, stumbling slightly over the word *Coliseum*.

"Look at that wall! It reminds me of Wood Rose," said Jennifer sitting next to her.

"That's Vatican City," said Carolina, trying to concentrate on not getting in an accident. "Dara, are we supposed to turn anywhere?"

Dara, who was sitting in the passenger seat next to Carolina, spread out the map on her lap. "According to the directions that Senora De Rossa gave you, we are supposed to be heading south if we want to go to Frascati." She glanced out the window and saw the Coliseum again. "We have already been this way, Carolina."

"I know, I think I am going in circles. We need to find a highway that takes us south out of the city."

Dara pointed to a small spot on the map. "We are supposed to turn left at the traffic lights along Via Enrico Fermi."

"Why is everyone honking their horns?" Carolina passed the Coliseum once again and then turned left at some traffic lights.

"After approximately one kilometer, you will pass the traffic lights at the ENEA complex." Dara looked out the window. "Then keep straight on for 200 meters and then turn right onto the road that runs between a FIAT dealer and the Tor Vergata train station."

"How provincial!" said Carolina. All the FIGs watched for the train station.

"Here it is." Carolina made the right turn, and they soon found themselves in the country. "Well that was certainly an adventure," Carolina said taking a deep breath. The city, along with most of the traffic, was now behind them, and for the next 10 minutes they were able to relax and enjoy the beautiful Italian countryside.

Jennifer was the first to spot the sign indicating that Frascati was ahead. Then, just beyond, towering on a hill in the distance, they saw it. The Villa Mondragone.

"Oh ... my ... gosh," said Carolina.

After several more minutes, with additional maps and directions, they parked in front of what could only be described as a large country farm house, with impatiens, peonies, and marigolds spilling from wooden flower boxes, a substantial vegetable garden off to one side, and toward the back, a barn complete with cows. There were other out buildings as well. Chickens were scratching in a fenced-off area near the barn, and from the top of a fence post nearby a rooster crowed. Carolina looked at the address Senora De Rossa had given her. "Maybe I wrote it down wrong," she said. "This hardly looks like an apartment."

They watched as the large wooden front doors to the villa opened, and a smiling elderly couple poured out. Behind them was another woman, slightly younger, a little on the stout side, and all smiles. "Welcome, welcome!" Carolina recognized the voice. It was Senora De Rossa.

Carolina and the FIGs had arrived.

Chapter Eleven

*I*t was almost dark when Lyuba returned from the village. Her potions had sold well and several women who had been shopping asked to have their palms read. It was usually the women who asked; men didn't believe, or if they did, they wouldn't admit it.

She walked into camp and nodded to the other women who had already returned. The riders. They didn't understand the value of walking. It was no wonder they didn't know where to find the best herbs; they saw nothing but the back of a truck.

She had found a four-leaf clover that morning on the way to the village—a sign of good luck. She had also found a 10 lire coin on the street where she had set up to sell her medicinals. She spat on it for good luck. A feeling of contentment was her companion this evening, something she had not experienced in a long while. That feeling gave way to alarm, however, as she approached her hut. In the large elm a magpie was chattering; a bad omen. As soon as she entered the door, she knew. Someone had been there in her absence.

She stood still in the middle of the room listening, sniffing the air, feeling the air on her bare skin. Her eyes searched. Behind the curtain, now partially open, on the shelf where she kept her medicinals she noticed. Two of the bottles had been disturbed; dried herbs had been taken. She immediately knew which ones. Ephedra and flitwort, healing herbs if used properly, but dangerous otherwise. Flitwort would cause severe mouth ulcers. But the ephedra, if misused, could be deadly. Not even a *parik-til* could offer protection against it.

She looked at the other shelves; the bottles and jars were as she had left them. Then she noticed the photograph of her precious child. It had been moved. Someone had picked it up to look at it more closely. The lock of hair that she had carefully cut from the head of her beautiful baby had been violated. She picked up the photograph and pressed it to her breast as rage filled her body. Only one person would dare enter her hut when she was not present and touch her things. This time he had gone too far. She would teach Milosh a lesson he would never forget.

She washed herself with the water she had collected earlier that morning from the nearby spring; it calmed her. Then she went outside to join the others by the fire. There was a mood of celebration, for the Bandoleer had returned to camp with a cow and its calf, the reason for his leaving in the darkness of night. That meant there would be fresh milk for the younger children. She sat down next to Djidjo, Milosh's mother, and spread out her full skirt around her.

"Milosh will soon be a man," she said, looking deeply into the eyes of the other woman. "It is time he learned more of the ancient healing and remedies. With your permission, I would like for him to join me in the morning when I go to collect my herbs." Lyuba smiled. She knew that by asking permission, Djidjo would agree. She was filled with false pride. She expected recognition and respect where she deserved none.

"I was wondering when you would see how smart he is." Her tone was boastful. "He has the makings of the next Bandoleer, perhaps the next Gypsy King. You should teach him all you know."

Lyuba anticipated such a remark and held her tongue. "I will expect him at my hut tomorrow morning one hour before dawn."

Djidjo nodded. It would be difficult to get her son up that early and he would complain, but she would do it. After all, Lyuba had singled him out over all the others. She would teach him the ancient gypsy magic. How proud his father would be.

The next morning, Lyuba sat in the darkness just outside her hut watching and waiting. A few minutes before the time he was expected, she saw Milosh stumble out of his parents' trailer and head in her direction.

* * *

Carolina and the FIGs had no trouble settling in at the farmhouse. Senor and Senora Granchelli immediately embraced them, taking them in like they were family. Since both Carolina and Dara spoke Italian, there was little difficulty in communicating with their hosts, who could speak only a little English, and translating for Jennifer and Mackenzie.

For some reason, meeting Senora De Rossa for the first time was a little unnerving for Carolina. The senora soon put her at ease as she wrapped her ample arms around her. "Please, we have known each other for several years now, talking by telephone. You must call me Lucia. No more of this Senora De Rossa."

Senora De Rossa—Lucia—was a distant cousin of Senor and Senora Granchelli, the visitors soon learned. Either a second cousin or third cousin twice removed, they weren't sure. And even after several minutes of enthusiastically discussing it, they still couldn't resolve it. Either way, they were family; and now, Carolina and the FIGs would be considered family as well. The rooms that had been prepared for them were spacious, private, and took up the entire second floor of the three-story farmhouse. There were three beds made up in the largest room, which had two windows overlooking the barn, the chicken house, and nearby pastures. This is where Dara, Mackenzie, and Jennifer would sleep. "I thought you would be more comfortable if you shared this room." Senora Granchelli smiled at the young girls she now considered her own. Another bedroom had been prepared for Carolina. It also had two windows; these overlooked the vegetable garden and the vineyards beyond. Besides the two bedrooms, there was a bathroom down the hall, and a comfortable private sitting area. Vases filled with freshly cut white lavender were prominently displayed in each room, making Carolina and the FIGs feel special.

Something else Carolina noticed, as did Jennifer since she had the eye of an artist, was Senora Granchelli's color scheme throughout her home: bright, happy colors of dark blue, burnt orange, and goldenrod yellow. It was the same as what Carolina had chosen for her bungalow.

The Granchelli home, farm, and vineyard were situated several kilometers off the main road that ran between the village of Frascati and the Villa Mondragone. "When the weather is clear," Senora Granchelli explained, "you can see the Old Villa from your window, Carolina." The fact that she used the ancient name for the Villa Mondragone intrigued Carolina.

Several generations of Granchellis had been born and reared in the old farmhouse, brought up to tend the fields, raise the food and livestock they needed for their own use, and produce wine from the vineyards to sell. Two of the Granchelli children, both daughters, had left the farm, preferring to find their own way outside of farm life. The ones who had stayed, however, three sons now with their own families, had built homes on the sprawling property, close enough to do the work necessary to maintain the farm and vineyard, but far enough away to allow privacy. "It is all we have ever known," Senora

Granchelli spoke with pride. "Even after Frascati outgrows its borders and tourists flock from all over the world to taste our fine wines, the Granchellis will still be here farming and making wine. That is what we do."

Lucia couldn't stop looking at Carolina as Senora Granchelli showed her and the three girls around. Remembering her as that frightened little girl, and now seeing her as a young woman, was almost heart wrenching. There was so much she wanted to tell her, but this was not the time. For now she must be content to know that the child of the gypsy woman had returned.

"All of you must eat," Senora Granchelli instructed. "Airplane food is terrible." This from a woman who had never traveled farther than the village of Frascati. "I have a little something prepared. Then you must rest. And then you can go about your business tomorrow. Mother Granchelli knows about these things."

And so Senora Granchelli became Mother Granchelli after only a few minutes. And Senor Granchelli insisted on being called Papa. After all, Carolina was about the same age as his youngest daughter—one of the ungrateful children who had decided to leave the farm—something that had yet to be forgiven. Mother Granchelli clucked her tongue and shook her head. It was a subject that still caused hard feelings and, therefore, it should be dropped. But Papa had several other stories he could tell. The little something turned out to be a feast that only an Italian mother in the old country can prepare. Even Lucia, who was used to Mother Granchelli's ways, was amazed.

"I think spaghetti is my favorite food," said Mackenzie helping herself to one of several home-made pasta dishes prepared by Mother Granchelli.

Dara and Jennifer nodded their agreement, their mouths too full to speak. With all of the excitement, none of the girls had felt hungry when they first arrived at the Granchelli's. But now, with the wonderful smells of home cooking and surrounded by friendly chatter, each in her own mind thought of family. This was how it was supposed to be.

When at last they finished eating, everyone helped clean up. It was then that Lucia told Carolina she had scheduled some time off from her job, and that she would be happy to show Carolina and the FIGs, which Dara had explained was not pejorative but rather a term of affection, around. But only if they wanted her to, for her intention was not to interfere. "Perhaps I could make proper introductions at the Old Villa," she suggested, thereby making their business there a little easier. Of course, Carolina gratefully accepted.

"Enough business talk," scolded Mother Granchelli. "All of you must rest until tomorrow. Tomorrow you can start your work, but not until. Today, you must rest." She was so insistent that Carolina and the girls had little choice. They took naps, walked through the pastures and fields, explored the barns, and admired the grapes with Papa Granchelli that would soon be ripe for picking. "This is our best year yet," said Papa with a wink.

That night, after eating more food than any one of them ever dreamed possible, Dara, Mackenzie, and Jennifer said goodnight. They were more quiet than usual as they dressed for bed in the room covered in wallpaper of yellow cabbage-patch roses and scented with white lilacs; the room chosen especially for them. Each girl was lost in her own thoughts, once again playing the game what if and why; and being forever grateful that Carolina was one of them. Otherwise, they wouldn't have been given this opportunity. Tomorrow they would get down to business, but for this one night—the end to the most perfect day they had ever experienced, because it was the closest thing they had ever experienced to having a real family—they would hold onto it for as long as they could, remembering each word, each look, each touch, each gesture ... each expression of love.

* * *

Mrs. Ball sorted through the incoming mail, organizing it, as she always did, with the largest pieces on the bottom and the smallest pieces on top. The three small envelopes, each with a different style of handwriting addressed to "THE Headmaster Thurgood James Harcourt," caught her sharp intuitive eye, and it was those envelopes that she placed on the very top. With the sorting finished, she carried the pile of mail into Dr. Harcourt's office and placed it front and center on his massive desk where he could attend to it once he arrived. He liked to take care of his mail first, before starting on other important matters, so she always made sure he would see it first.

"Good morning, Mrs. Ball."

Mrs. Ball jumped, nearly spilling the cup of coffee she had just poured for herself. Dr. Harcourt's new-found cheerfulness was something Mrs. Ball was struggling with since it was so uncharacteristic of the headmaster. It was taking a little getting used to. She gritted her teeth, set her jaw, and responded in what she hoped was an equally cheerful mood. "Good morning, Dr. Harcourt." Then, just in case all of that cheerfulness had clouded his eyesight, she added, "Your mail is on your desk."

Dr. Harcourt smiled. "Another beautiful day," and he disappeared into his office. Once there, he immediately went to the large, multi-paned window flanked by dark green draperies so he could examine any possible signs of new growth on his prize *Photinia fraseri*. There had been a nice soaking rain during the night, and with the extra warm day-time temperatures, plus a healthy dose of fertilizer that had been spread by the grounds crew, he expected to see nubs, if not actual leaves, any day now. There was nothing. But that didn't alter the sheer joy he felt on this third day without the FIGs at Wood Rose.

He noticed the stack of mail. He also noticed the small envelopes neatly piled on top. There appeared to be three of them. The handwriting on the envelope most visible was large, bold, and in all capitals. His new-found feeling of euphoria started to crinkle slightly around the edges. Out of habit more than anything else, he rubbed the side of his head. He hesitated for only a moment, then, determined not to let anything spoil this beautiful morning, he grabbed the envelope and slit it open with a gift from a previous graduating class of seniors—the sterling silver opener that had been recently encased in aluminum foil.

He read through the note several times, managing to pick out and translate only a few of the words that had been written in a language with which he was unfamiliar. *Apologia* was one of the words he managed to translate; a picture of what appeared to be hieroglyphs of an eyeball with a single tear for another. It was signed *DARA ROUX*.

The next envelope, addressed to him in a neat, slanted cursive, proved to be a bit of a puzzle as well. Mathematical formula written inside an elongated cube made absolutely no sense at all. However, there was included a key on the bottom of the note, which he didn't totally understand, but he was at least able to decipher two words: *I apologize*. It was signed Mackenzie Yarborough.

Feeling a little less anxious, he picked up the third envelope. Even if he hadn't already guessed who it was from, he would have known from the large, loopy lettering that slanted backwards. He slit open the envelope and pulled out the small note paper. On it was a picture of his *Photinia fraseri* painted in pastels, before it had been whacked. She had even managed to capture the true shade of blush on the tips of its many leaves. It was signed Jennifer Torres, with curvilinear vowels and a small circle placed over the letter *i*. The headmaster sighed. They had apologized—in their own way—but apologized nonetheless. At least that's what he thought the notes were. Then, for the second time in just a matter of days, he broke out in song. This time Mrs. Ball didn't call security.

Chapter Twelve

"Why do you have to pick herbs so early in the morning?" grumbled Milosh. Without answering, Lyuba walked determinedly on a dirt path bordered by overgrown weeds that were once part of a magnificent garden on the grounds of the Old Villa. She was looking for something special this morning, and she knew where to find it.

Milosh stomped along behind Lyuba, taking no care of flora that might serve some beneficial purpose later. "How much farther do we have to go?" It had angered him when his mother woke him so early. Just when he was having the dream that proved he was a man. He wondered if Lyuba even knew what she was doing. She was getting old. She needed to be replaced as the *choovihni*—something he had mentioned to his father—someone younger who would respect him as the son of the Bandoleer. He had not mentioned that. He smirked as he thought about the herbs he had stolen from her hut. And the hair. She had better treat him better or he would show her a thing or two.

Lyuba stopped at the ancient live oak growing near the stream. A clump of Monkshood grew near an exposed root. Careful not to disturb the plant, she sat down and waited for Milosh to catch up.

"Sit here beside me, Milosh," she told him.

He glanced around warily. What was the old woman doing now?

"I have told you many times that everything has a soul. Rocks, plants, even the far-away stars and planets. Do you believe that?"

"I guess." Not giving it much thought, he scratched at his arm, wishing it was a little lighter so he could see her face. He thought he had been careful inside her hut, putting everything back the way he had found it. If she knew, though, she would have already confronted his father. No. He had gotten away with it. Going into the place where another gypsy slept without being invited was taboo. To steal from another gypsy was even worse. He had done both and gotten away with it. He felt an excitement build within the pit of his stomach.

"I have also told you that everything is inherently good and, therefore, should be respected. It is only when things are not used for a good purpose that bad things happen." She waited for him to stop fidgeting. The sky was turning a light gray; the sun would reveal itself soon. "Take this little plant here." She pointed to the small plant with sparse blue flowers.

"What about it?" The ground where he sat was damp and had soaked through his trousers. His mother had told him Lyuba would teach him all of her ancient magic. Instead, she was yakking about some stupid plant.

Lyuba reached out and held her hand over one of the delicate flowers, careful not to touch it. "This tiny plant can make men strong and virile, and it can make women beautiful and desirable."

Finally. She was telling him something he needed to know. Milosh yanked off a couple of the flowers and sniffed them, then tasted them, just as Lyuba knew he would.

Quietly she waited. The first gentle rays of the sun appeared over the horizon. "It is called Monkshood or Friar's Cap," she explained, watching his face. "If not used properly, it can be deadly."

Milosh jumped up. "I just tasted it. What do

you mean it can be deadly?" He rubbed his head. "I don't feel too good. My lips are burning." His words were becoming slurred. "Can't talk right."

Lyuba watched him. "Little boys shouldn't go where they do not belong or play with things that don't belong to them."

Then he understood. Lyuba somehow found out that he had taken some of her herbs. Maybe she even knew he had taken that hair. "You have poisoned me," he tried to say, but his tongue felt like it was too big for his mouth.

"I didn't poison you, Milosh. You poisoned yourself with your greed, your thoughts, and your actions—all negative. You think only of yourself. That is why you feel the way you do now. The little blue flower only reacts to the bad. If you had good thoughts and performed good deeds, the little blue flower would make you strong and virile.

He stood up and clumsily staggered over to the water where he tried to stoop down and wash his face. He vomited instead.

Lyuba removed a white handkerchief from her pocket and untied the knot to expose a small root from the sassafras. It would neutralize the alkaloid and aconitine of the blue flower. But first she wanted to make sure he understood.

"Milosh, you are in the singular position of being a leader of men one day. You must use your position to do good. Forget trying to harm others. It doesn't become the son of the Bandoleer. And it dishonors our tribe." She stood and walked over to where he lay. I will put your indiscretion behind me now, but be warned. If you ever do it again, I will call together a *kris*. At that time, I will insist on *marime*. You will be a disgrace to yourself, your family, and to your tribe; and you will be banished."

Milosh lay on the ground too sick to say anything. He wasn't too sick to understand her words, though. The *kris* was like a gypsy court of law, and if the old woman got her way, he would be forced to leave the tribe. That's what *marime* was.

"Suck on this." She handed him the root. "It will ease your cramps and restore feeling in your mouth and limbs." Then she left. She didn't want to be there when the poison flushed through his intestines. He could find his own way home once the nausea passed and he felt stronger.

* * *

Carolina awoke feeling completely refreshed and eager to start the day. She quickly dialed Larry's cell phone number. Not getting an answer, she left a message similar to the one she had left when they first landed—she and the FIGs had arrived safely and were comfortably installed in a beautiful, rustic Italian farmhouse. She would call again later.

Before going to bed the night before, she and the FIGs had discussed their plans and decided to visit the Villa Mondragone first. With any luck, and with Lucia along to help smooth their way through the system at the Second University of Rome, the university that now owned the Villa Mondragone, they would be able to examine other books and private collections in the library that were from the same period as the Voynich Manuscript.

Carolina found the bathroom down the hall empty. Even though the house was old, everything seemed to be in surprisingly good order. The shower was even better than the one in her bathroom at the bungalow. Not wanting to disturb the FIGs—they were probably exhausted from the trip—she quickly dressed and tiptoed down the stairs to the kitchen.

"The hardest part was wrapping each one of those paperclips." Jennifer was telling the story to Mother Granchelli and Papa in English, and Dara was rapidly translating. "And then unwrapping them." Mackenzie stood at the stove preparing what looked like gigantic omelets. Everyone was laughing.

"My gosh. Did I oversleep?"

Mother Granchelli jumped up and hugged her newest daughter. "We are hearing about Wood Rose," she said. "Such a nice place."

"Yes." Carolina glanced at the FIGs and sat down at the table. She had never seen them look more relaxed—and happy. "Maybe you and Papa can come visit some time."

"Mother Granchelli and Papa have fresh eggs—from chickens!" Mackenzie was obviously enjoying the farm aspect of where they were staying. "Papa even let me gather the eggs this morning." She flopped another whopping omelet onto a plate and set it in front of Carolina.

"Papa is going to take us for a ride on his tractor to see the rest of the farm," added Dara, "later this evening when we get back from Villa Mondragone." She poured a cup of coffee and set it in front of Carolina.

Carolina nodded and then looked at all the food on the table. "I can't believe I am hungry again, after all that we ate last night."

"It is the country air, Carolina." Mother Granchelli smiled at the newest additions to her family. "I will see that all of you have rosy cheeks before you return to Wood Rose. Too much work—all that worry—is not good. Here, you will relax, eat, and have a good time."

A few minutes later, Lucia arrived and joined them in the kitchen. She looked more rested than she had on the previous day; she didn't seem quite so solemn. Mackenzie jumped up from the table and began cooking her an omelet as well. "I was able to get in touch with Rector Catoni at the Old Villa last evening to ask his permission for you to examine the library. The students are on break now, so it is a perfect time for you to go. He asked that I tell you he is looking forward to meeting you, and will be at your service for whatever you need. He is a nice man, Carolina. You will like him."

Without any warning, Carolina's eyes filled with tears. This had been a long journey, which started when she first learned she was adopted. Now she was closer than she had ever been to finding out who she was and where she had come from. The three FIGs had never seen Carolina cry. Jennifer covered her face with her hands, and Mackenzie burst out bawling. Dara simply looked away.

"What is this? *I ragazzi*," Mother Granchelli scolded. One by one she pulled the young women into her embrace and wiped each face with her apron. "I told you too much work is a bad thing. Now, Mother Granchelli will get out the grape jelly—made from the grapes of our vineyards. It is good on my fresh-baked *pane filoncino* and will go well with Mackenzie's omelets. Sit! Now eat!"

Carolina and the FIGs ate the grape jelly on the warm crusty bread. It did make them feel better. Soon they were chattering away once again, speaking in Italian with Dara, who was translating for Jennifer and Mackenzie, all of them laughing. Only Lucia remained somewhat subdued, tentative. She knew what the tears meant, and it made her all the more determined to do whatever she could to help the child of the gypsy woman.

Chapter Thirteen

Lyuba quickly returned to camp. On the way, a single crow flew down and landed on the path in front of her. Another bad omen. Back at her hut, she gathered the things she wished to take into the village to sell that day. Her heart was heavy, for she knew that Milosh had once again chosen to follow the darkness of his heart and ignore her warnings.

Milosh angrily pushed through the underbrush, not seeing the path that was before him. The old woman had embarrassed him. He would make her sorry.

Back at the camp he hid in the trees until he saw his mother and father leave. He didn't want to answer their questions. Not now. Then he went into the trailer and removed the book of curses from the trunk. He had learned a lot from reading the book.

He knew what he wanted to do.

With Bakro forgotten for another day, he reached under the pallet that was his bed where he slept and pulled out the herbs and strands of hair he had taken from Lyuba's hut. Then he mixed them in a jar he found in his mother's cabinet. He didn't know who the little girl was in the photograph, but she must be someone important to Lyuba. Using all of his negative emotions—the hurt, hate, frustration and fear—he felt a tingling electricity within his body and in the air around him. The curse was working. Lyuba had called him a little boy. She would be taught to respect him as the man that he was. The ancient gypsy magic wasn't just knowledge. It was being brave enough to use it. And he was brave.

Once he was sure the herbs and hair were mixed well, he tossed the jar under his pallet, hidden from view. Then he lay down, still weak from the Monkshood, and fell into a black, dreamless sleep.

* * *

Since Lucia wouldn't spend the entire day at the Villa Mondragone, she drove her own car. Carolina and the FIGs followed behind in their rental. The villa towered on a hill before them. Once there, they parked in a reserved parking area. "It's 416 meters above sea level. The estate consists of an 18-hectare lot," Mackenzie informed them as all of them gaped at the magnificent structure. "The villa itself is about 80,000 cubic metres, and it faces Rome."

Lucia smiled. "You girls have done your homework."

"Look," said Carolina. "You can see the farm from here." Off in the distance a little north of the villa, the Granchelli farmhouse and barns were visible, as well as the vineyards. Carolina wanted to absorb everything about this ancient place—its sounds, its smells, its position in relation to the things nearby. Behind the villa slightly to the west, she could just make out what looked to be some small trailers and a few make-shift huts. "What is that, Lucia?"

"It is the gypsy camp," she answered.

Immediately Carolina felt a chill. Lucia put her arm around her.

"It is the black tribe. They have been gone for many years, but only just recently returned."

"How long will they stay?" Dara asked. She and the other FIGs remembered what Lucia had told Carolina about her last name, Lovel, and its connection to the black tribe.

"Only they know that. They will stay until they feel it is no longer beneficial for them to remain. When they feel it is time to leave, they will. One day they will simply be gone." Lucia took Carolina by the arm and led her toward the villa. "Come. I'll introduce you to Rector Catoni. I know he is eager to tell you of the villa's history."

Rector Catoni was much younger than Carolina or the FIGs expected. "I thought he would be an old guy," whispered Dara.

"Yeah, wearing a monk's robe," added Jennifer.

Mackenzie gave Rector Catoni the once over and told the others, "This guy is kinda cute." Carolina tried to look stern at the three girls, but giggled instead. After all, he was young, and he was cute. Wavy dark hair, dark eyes, a nice smile, good build. And charming.

"So, Ms. Lovel ..." He took her hand and caressed it.

"Please call me Carolina."

The FIGs giggled.

"You are researching the Voynich Manuscript?"

"Yes. And any other documents that might be from that same period."

The three FIGs, Carolina, and Lucia made

themselves comfortable on the Louis XVI sofa and chairs covered in dark purple velvet, the color of royalty, nobility, and spirituality, in the seating area of Rector Catoni's office. The room was about the size of the cafeteria at Wood Rose. High ceilings, tall windows, massive furniture, heavy fabrics, reflective of a time long past, and beautifully aged with historical importance. There was a light tap on the door, and another slightly younger man entered, carrying a coffee service on a large silver tray.

"Another hottie," whispered Dara to the other FIGs. All three giggled. Carolina cleared her throat.

"I thought you might like some coffee," Rector Catoni said, "before you start to work."

The young hottie served the coffee while the rector explained more of the history of the villa. "Between 1616 and 1618 significant works of enlargement of Villa Mondragone were carried out under the direction of the Flemish architect Jan van Santen. These interventions affected both the block enlarged with the gallery between the Casino of Longhi and the Retirata, the small residential building constructed for the son of Cardinal Altemps, and the external part of the great garden, the portico, and the large quadrangular courtyard, which is near where you parked."

Carolina listened carefully, hoping to pick up on something in his words and gestures that would trigger a long-ago memory. There was something—a flicker—when he mentioned the garden. But just as quickly, it disappeared. Nothing else that he said was even remotely familiar to her except for what she herself had uncovered during her research. She wanted to explore the library.

Knowing Carolina was eager to get started, and also knowing the rector could talk about the villa indefinitely without any encouragement, Lucia put her cup back on the silver tray and stood, deliberately gathering her pocket book and car keys. "Rector Catoni, I must be going now. If you will be so kind as to show my friends to the library ..." She glanced at Carolina and smiled.

"Of course." He made a slight movement under his desk and immediately the hottie returned. "Alfonso will show you to the library and be available to help you for as long as you need. If I can personally be of service, please ... Perhaps tomorrow you will allow me to show you more of the estate."

"Thank you, Rector Catoni. You have been more than generous with your time."

Lucia smiled at Carolina and because her heart went out to her, she reached out and hugged her.

"Mother Granchelli has invited me for supper. Shall we plan to meet back at the farm by six o'clock?"

"That will be wonderful," said Carolina. "We'll see you there. Thank you."

Alfonso led Carolina and the FIGs down the hall and through several connecting rooms, all the while explaining the significance of the different rooms and artifacts within, until they reached the older part of the villa. "It is generally accepted that the Voynich Manuscript was part of a larger collection belonging to the Collegio Romano that was transferred to the Villa Mondragone during the period following the Risorgimento," explained Alfonso.

"*Alfonso,*" Dara whispered to Mackenzie and Jennifer, "is derived from Visigothic *Adalfuns*. It means noble. And ready." She arched her right eyebrow, causing the others to giggle once again.

Alfonso smiled at the girls. "That was in 1870 when Italy was unified, then secularized. Just prior to that, Don Marcantonio Borghese, owner of the Villa Mondragone, signed an agreement with the Jesuits to use the villa as a college for the Italian nobility." He paused in front of an archway leading to a large room filled with books. "This is the *Bibliotheca Major*, which is the main library. The private library, however, which is called the *Bibliotheca Secreta*, is where the private collections have always been kept. It is where the Voynich Manuscript was discovered." He walked past several more rooms until he reached the separate library.

Alfonso left once he saw that Carolina and her students were situated, and for the next several hours, Carolina and the FIGs went through old books, manuscripts, loose papers and documents. Just trying to absorb the work in front of them was overwhelming. There were literally hundreds of books and stacks of papers, seemingly in some sort of order, but the order was not immediately discernable.

Mackenzie, because of her special talent for deciphering codes and solving problems, was the first to suggest how to accomplish the most out of what was obviously going to be a gargantuan task. "We need to divide the room into fourths: then work from top to bottom, left to right. If we find anything that looks remotely helpful, we will pull it, mark the spot where we took it from with a sheet of paper with its name or any other identification, and put it aside to examine later. Once we have pulled everything we want to take a closer look at, we will start going through each one more thoroughly."

It made sense. Otherwise, it would be too easy

to get confused and overlook something critical. Carolina and the FIGs began work in earnest. Several times Alfonso unobtrusively popped his head in to ask if they needed anything. Refreshments? Help with moving heavy books?

They were fine.

Finally, exhausted and covered in dust, with no idea of how long they had been working, they stopped. Carolina glanced at her watch. It was already 5:30. They needed to return to the farm. She looked around her. Only a few things worth a second look had been pulled from the shelves. That wasn't especially encouraging, but they had only gone through about a fraction of what was in the library. This was turning into a much bigger project than she had anticipated. Tomorrow they would get an early start, and with any luck at all, by the end of the week they would know what needed to be examined more closely.

* * *

Mrs. Ball just couldn't seem to break herself from being startled every time Dr. Harcourt said good morning to her in that new, cheerful, high-pitched voice. It just sounded so aberrant. This time she dropped the mail on the floor. "Good morning, Dr. Harcourt," she answered as she bent over to scoop up what was intended for his desk. He had arrived early, and she hadn't been prepared for him.

"Anything interesting in the mail?" he asked.

She looked at him in disbelief. He actually missed the FIGs. All the complaining he had done over the years, all of the pranks he had been subjected to, all of the aspirin she had given him to sooth his migraines, and he actually missed them.

She stood up and gathered her composure. "Nothing from Carolina," she said, breaking her self-imposed rule of always referring to faculty as Mr., Ms., or Mrs., "or the FIGs," breaking another rule by not calling the FIGs by their given names, "if that is what you mean." He really was starting to irritate her.

"Oh, I wasn't expecting anything from them," he said quickly. A little too quickly from the way Mrs. Ball saw it.

"I do have the address and phone number where they are staying," she offered in an attempt to match his cheerful manner.

"Oh, no. I wouldn't want to interfere with their research." And he went into his office, closing the door before Mrs. Ball could gather up all the mail and put it on his desk.

She sighed, then knocked and entered. He was standing in front of the multi-paned window, shoulders more stooped than usual, staring at the *Photinia fraseri*.

"I believe I saw some new growth," she said as she placed the headmaster's mail front and center on his desk.

Either he didn't hear her, or he didn't wish to comment. Not feeling the least bit cheerful, she left, closing the door firmly behind her.

Dr. Harcourt had also noticed the new growth and that pleased him. What didn't please him was the feeling that Wood Rose had suddenly become a dull haven for all who were associated with it, himself included, in spite of his initial euphoria. The natural cheerfulness he had experienced with the departure of the FIGs was now unnatural and somewhat on the forced side. The faculty and staff seemed moody and sullen, and Mrs. Ball was starting to get downright snippy. Even Ms. Alcott, a frequent visitor whose well-known acid tongue and strong opinions had reddened his ears with regularity over the years, didn't want to come around now that the FIGs weren't on campus. "It's just too quiet and boring," she had told him the day before after a board meeting. "You are a pompous stuffed shirt, and you run this place like a funeral parlor." She was right. It was too quiet—*and* boring. Not only that, as difficult as it was to admit, he was a pompous stuffed shirt. And even the appearance of the soft blush of red tips couldn't alter that fact.

Chapter Fourteen

*L*yuba spent a good part of the day in the
village selling her medicinals, reading palms, and
paying special attention to the appearance of omens.
Ever since the unfortunate incident with Milosh,
a feeling of darkness was engulfing her that she
couldn't shake. Before leaving Milosh at the spring
that morning, she had made another offering: a
coin thrown into the water. For extra protection,
she had tied her hanky to the branch of an ancient
oak. Later, while walking the streets of Frascati, she
sought comfort by rubbing her stone, her own lucky
charm. That had helped calm her somewhat, but only
temporarily.

Oddly, two crows had approached her on
her way back to the camp that evening, a sign of
joy. Yet the black feeling still remained. She didn't

understand this dichotomy of foretelling. Both good and bad signs were revealing themselves, a contradiction of things to come. How could this be? She would have to be extra vigilant. As soon as she returned to her hut she would prepare a special *duk rak*, her own psychic shield. Perhaps that would ease her anxiety.

* * *

"What do you think of Lucia?" As usual, it was Dara who easily identified and then brought up important matters that were on the collective minds of the FIGs. After working at the library all day, and then helping Mother Granchelli clean up after eating, the girls had gone for a ride around the farm on Papa's tractor, just as he had promised. By the time they got back to the house, it was dark. It had been a long day, and they were starting to feel the delayed reaction of jetlag. Carolina had gone upstairs to her room earlier, and they soon followed.

"She's always around, isn't she?" commented Jennifer. "Watching Carolina."

"Yeah, I noticed that, too." Mackenzie stuck one leg out from under the dark blue cotton spread on her bed like a thermometer. It allowed her to enjoy the soft fragrant covers without getting too hot. "I get the feeling she really cares about Carolina. I just can't figure out why. I mean, sure, she was involved in Carolina's adoption. And they have talked several times on the phone. But ..."

"I know what you mean. It's like she has an unnatural interest in Carolina." Dara stared up at the ceiling, the tallest ceiling she had ever seen, other than the ceilings at the Villa Mondragone. Unlike the villa, however, here there were no cracks and they weren't painted in gold. "Carolina told us that Lucia wasn't involved in her actual adoption; only that she had just started working with the agency at that time." Dara lifted up on one elbow and looked at the other two FIGs. "She knows a whole lot more than she has told Carolina, and she feels guilty about something."

Mackenzie sat up in bed. "I agree. Now, maybe by meeting Carolina, she will be more open with her—and tell her what she knows."

Jennifer flipped her ponytail. "Tomorrow we should give the two of them some time alone together so if Lucia does want to tell her anything, she can."

"I agree," said Dara.

"Me, too," added Mackenzie.

The three girls settled back into the soft sheets and comforters of their beds, thinking. Thinking about Carolina, the new things they would discover in the days ahead, and their own dreams of what the future would bring.

* * *

Carolina had intended to stay up a little longer, at least until Papa and the FIGs returned from their tractor ride, but found herself feeling especially tired after eating Mother Granchelli's delicious supper of stuffed manicotti, garlic bread, salad, and tiramisu for dessert. After trying to call Larry and again getting no answer, she took a long, hot shower to mull over all that they needed to accomplish over the next several days. Feeling slightly warm, she opened one of the windows in her room before getting into bed. Within minutes, she fell asleep, but repeatedly reawakened until one dream finally absorbed all of the others: the dream of a young child in a beautiful garden; a little girl with large green eyes, screaming in terror.

Chapter Fifteen

"Do you read the Tarot cards?" The question was from a young gentleman, well dressed, straight white teeth, clean nails, uncalloused hands. The shape of his head, and the way he presented his words; Lyuba guessed he was a scholar. She wondered when he would ask. He had been watching her for some time. Even so, she was surprised by his interest, especially the Tarot. Judging from his clothes, she guessed he was an American.

In answer to his question she smiled, then reached into the basket for her deck of Tarot cards wrapped in black silk. Expertly and with obvious familiarity she first spread out the black silk in which they had been wrapped, then the cards on the soft grass in front of her. "Please," she motioned for him to sit opposite her.

The place where the gypsy sat had been picked with much deliberation. It was where she would be seen by anyone with an interest or a desire to learn that which was hidden, and the branches from the full-leafed red maple provided shade and comfort. Plus it was near the government building. It was her favorite spot.

The young man watched the gypsy's hands as she shuffled, then touched each card. The cards themselves were well cared for but old and unlike any others he had ever seen. "You don't use the Witches Tarot or the Norse," he commented.

"Those are for the charlatans," she answered. With great dexterity, she continued moving the cards, which were covered in colorful designs and details. Then she separated the cards into the major arcane and the minor arcane. She began with the simple nine-card Gypsy oracle, three rows of three. "The top row is the past, the center is the present, the bottom row is what's to come," she said. "But, of course, you know that, don't you?"

The man smiled.

She first studied the cards. Then she moved her hands over them, not touching them, but feeling the *zee*—that primeval intelligence giving all life and form energy. Satisfied, she picked them up. "Shuffle them, please."

He did as she instructed and returned the cards to her, watching her eyes as he did.

Once again she placed the cards one by one onto the black silk. Much to her surprise, they felt warm. The Magician, showing the man's qualifications; the High Priestess, indicating secrets not ready to be revealed; the Lovers, in this case a departure from the old and familiar toward something new and exciting.

She studied his face, and then placed three more cards down: the card showing strength; the Wheel of Fortune, indicating change; and then the card of Death, which in this case indicated the end of something in his life to make room for something new.

Then she placed down the final three cards: the Tower, meaning an unexpected blow; the Star of luck and hope for future happiness; and the last card, Temperance. He would need to be watchful and take special care.

Relying on her instinctive psychic powers, she asked him to select two cards from those which had not yet been chosen. Without hesitation he picked the cards and handed them to her. The first was the Seven of Wands. There were difficulties ahead requiring all of his endurance and strength to overcome. The other was the World card. She smiled. He would face a difficult challenge, but in the end, he would achieve all that he would need for contentment and satisfaction.

He nodded and handed her a 100,000 lire note. "Thank you, Mrs. Lovel." Then he left.

Lyuba was stunned. How had the man known her name? Only the members of her tribe knew it. She slipped the note into her pocket and quickly gathered the cards, carefully wrapping them in the black silk cloth. She would not remain in the village all day as she usually did. She needed to return to the camp.

* * *

Rector Catoni and Alfonso greeted Carolina and the FIGs when they arrived early that morning. "With all the students gone on their spring break, we are glad to have you visit us," the rector gushed, once again caressing Carolina's hand. Alfonso immediately took them back to the library where they had spent the day before. He had already prepared coffee and left it for them to serve themselves whenever they wanted it.

"I really like that guy," said Mackenzie when Alfonso left. She put the third spoon-full of sugar into her cup of back coffee.

Dara handed Jennifer the small pitcher of cream. "His dialect is interesting. He is well educated, but I would guess he comes from one of the islands where the main livelihood is from fishing."

Carolina sipped her coffee and looked around at what they had accomplished the day before. There was so much left to do. Maybe this hadn't been such a good idea after all. Maybe it was just the unobtainable wish of a silly child that she had nurtured and carried around with her all these years. Maybe she shouldn't have involved the FIGs. She felt tired, and they hadn't even gotten started.

"Don't worry, Carolina," said Jennifer, the most sensitive of the three FIGs and the most in tune to what other people were feeling. "We'll get it done."

Without further delay, they began pulling books from the shelves. A couple of times during the morning hours, Alfonso brought a fresh pot of coffee and refilled the sugar bowl and creamer. Not wishing to disturb the young women, he didn't linger. Carolina and the FIGs barely noticed, they were so engrossed in their task at hand. Then, from somewhere within the thick walls of the villa, a clock

Barbara Casey

began to strike. It was noon.

"Hello, girls." Lucia found them surrounded
by stacks of books and papers. She had brought
them lunch, something they weren't expecting, but
certainly appreciated. After washing the dust and
grime from their hands, they went outside to a
private courtyard to eat. A wrought iron table and
chairs had been provided, and it overlooked the
gardens, at least those that had been restored.

"This is just so beautiful," said Carolina,
admiring the vegetation, some of which was as old
as the villa itself. Her eyes paused for a moment on
a glint of sunlight coming through some trees; a
reflection from something at the gypsy camp. Like
the evening before, she felt uncomfortably warm.

"After those big meals Mother Granchelli
has been giving you, I thought you might enjoy a
lighter lunch of antipasto—prosciutto, cheese, olives,
melon, and, of course, some of Mother Granchelli's
homemade bread." Lucia poured each of them a
glass of wine. "From Papa's vineyard," she explained.
"I hope this is all right." She sought Carolina's
permission for the girls.

Carolina smiled and nodded. It was more than
all right. The food. The wine. None of the FIGs had
ever tasted wine, but Mother Granchelli served it

with all of the evening meals. After all, they were in Italy. It was the way it was supposed to be.

"Well, in that case ..." Dara giggled and held out her glass first.

As soon as they finished eating, Dara stood up from the table. "Carolina, do you mind if we take a walk before going back in? We won't be gone long." She looked at Mackenzie and Jennifer, signaling them that this was a good time to leave Carolina and Lucia alone. They understood.

"We'll be right back," said Jennifer.

Mackenzie followed. "I wonder where Alfonso is?" She repeated the name Alfonso just to make sure she said it clearly.

"Don't get lost." Carolina watched the three girls disappear around the corner of the stone wall.

"They are good girls," said Lucia, breaking the silence first.

"I know. I will really feel lost once they graduate. They are like little sisters to me."

"What will they do once they leave Wood Rose?"

It was like two old friends getting together after not seeing each other for awhile. They knew so much about each other. They had a history. Conversation came easily, and the natural affection they felt toward one another had only grown deeper now that they had finally met in person.

Carolina smiled. "They have many goals ahead of them," she answered. "Dara has been accepted at Yale University on a full scholarship. She wants to continue her studies in foreign languages and perhaps at some point go into the diplomatic service. Mackenzie, who you have probably noticed is a whiz at math, has been accepted into the Massachusetts Institute of Technology research program. Miss Alcott, one of our financial supporters at Wood Rose, is sponsoring her. I'm not sure where Mackenzie will land. Her problem-solving abilities spill over into human relationships as well. She is a peace-maker. She can do whatever she decides to do. And Jennifer will attend Juilliard when she isn't performing. She has already been received by the international world of music. Now they are just waiting for her reintroduction."

Carolina sipped her wine and leaned back in her chair. "I feel so blessed just to be a small part of their lives."

Lucia patted her hand. "They are also blessed to have you to care for them as you do."

"And you, Carolina. Do you have a young man in your life?"

"There is someone, but it's complicated."

"Love is always complicated. But if you find someone who is more important to you than anything else in the world, then it is right."

That was the problem, of course. She did love Larry and she couldn't imagine her life without him, but until she could find some sort of resolution to knowing who she was and where she came from—to feel at peace with it—he couldn't be the most important thing in her life.

Lucia studied Carolina and sensed her unrest. She wanted to tell Carolina about that awful day when that terrible man, Liruso, took her from her mother. She wanted to tell her how many times she had grieved over it, and how sorry she was. She also wanted to tell her that she had seen her mother only recently, and that it was her tribe camped nearby.

"Carolina … Sometimes we find ourselves in situations where we have no control."

Thinking Lucia was referring to the FIGs, Carolina laughed. "Believe me, where the FIGs are concerned, no one has control."

Lucia tried again. "I mean, sometimes lack of experience or youth makes us vulnerable. And even though we know something is wrong, we can do nothing about it." More than anything she wanted Carolina to understand. She prayed that she would forgive her for not doing more so many years ago.

Again, Carolina misunderstood. "Fortunately, all that the FIGs have done—their creative expressions—haven't caused any serious harm. They are such bright girls. Occasionally, they just need to vent. In fact," she turned toward the sound of the approaching giggling girls, "I would be willing to bet that Wood Rose is missing them right about now." She leaned forward so as not to be overheard, "Even Dr. Harcourt."

The three girls came into view, along with Alfonso. They had found him. The moment had passed.

After dinner that evening, Carolina excused herself because of fatigue. It had been another difficult day, but they had finished what they set out to do. They had gone through most of the private collections of the library. Once they finished what remained, they could sort through the materials they had pulled from the shelves—what little there was— and determine if any of it related to the Voynich Manuscript or to Carolina's special page.

Mother Granchelli clucked her tongue when Carolina left the kitchen. She didn't like the pale pallor to her face, or the darkness under her eyes. If she didn't feel better the next day, she would call the doctor in Frascati. She would not have one of her children sick. Meanwhile, she would fix a big pot of *zuppa di primavera* for the next day. It was what she had always prepared for her own children when they were growing up, and it had made them feel better. It would make Carolina feel better, too.

* * *

Carolina turned on the cold water in the shower. She just couldn't seem to get cool. It was probably the heat and humidity making her feel so tired. When she finished her shower, she dressed for bed.

She missed Larry. She wanted to talk to him and tell him about what they had been doing. It was time for final exams at the university. Either he was busy with those, or he just wasn't answering his phone. She had left several messages for him, but she didn't know if he had even gotten them.

She raised the window in her room and folded the covers at the foot of the bed before lying down. Maybe he had reached the point where he didn't want to wait for her any longer. Maybe this special project, which so consumed her, had finally driven him away and he had found someone else; someone who was willing to share herself with him completely. She had known he couldn't wait forever. But she thought at least he would have discussed it with her.

Maybe if she got a good night's sleep, she would feel better. She turned toward the open window, and off in the distance she saw the flickering light of a campfire. The gypsy campfire. After several minutes she got up and dug her cell phone out of her purse. It was 3 A.M. in Chapel Hill, but she really wanted to talk to him. She dialed the number. After several rings, his voice message answered. She hung up.

* * *

Dara put on her pajamas and climbed into bed. She had been right. Alfonso told them he was from the island of Marettimo, one of the Aegadian Islands just west of Sicily in the Mediterranean Sea. His father was a fisherman, and his mother made hand crafts to sell to tourists. The ancient name of the island, he had explained, was *Hiera*. Dara recognized that to be Spanish in origin, but it was also part of the Greek name, *Hiera Nesos*, which meant sacred island. The people who lived there believed the island to be the original Ithaca, location of Homer's

Odysseus. She loved this country with so much history.

While rummaging through the old books and documents earlier that day, she had discovered something she definitely wanted to look at more closely. It was an unbound manuscript that showed many similar script patterns and features such as the Voynich. Not identical, but similar. She would examine it first.

Late that afternoon, on their way back to the Granchelli farm from the villa, she had noticed a woman walking toward the gypsy camp carrying a basket. If the gypsies living in the camp were the black tribe, then it just made sense that Carolina should go visit them. Maybe they could tell her something. Did people even go visit gypsies? She wondered.

She also wondered, as she sometimes did, what her mother would think of her now, practically grown up, studying in Italy, soon to graduate from the Wood Rose Orphanage and Academy for Young Women. With the memory of ditch water tickling her feet, *You wait right here, I'll be back for you soon,* she fell asleep.

* * *

Jennifer finished brushing her hair and pulled it back with a scrunchy. They had accomplished a lot that day, and the job they had set out to do was more manageable now. It was nice of Lucia to bring them lunch. She wondered if she had talked to Carolina any more about her adoption.

Early that morning, before Carolina and the other FIGs had gotten up, she went out to the barn where Papa was milking a cow. She had never seen a cow being milked before; she had never even been on a farm before. Her parents had always lived in the city, close to where they worked. That evening after supper, Mother Granchelli let the FIGs help her make a big pot of soup, something she called *zuppa di primavera*. Jennifer had never cooked before, either. There had been hired people to take care of those things. She was experiencing so many new things.

Not that it worried her, but ever since arriving at the Granchelli farm, she hadn't heard the cadence. Other happy sounds of family and farm life seemed to take its place, until they were returning to the farm after working in the library all day. Suddenly she heard it again—loud and distinct. She had already sketched it in black and white with charcoals, and painted it in water colors. Now there was only the strong, defined beat. There had been nothing unusual going on at the time. Only a woman walking along the road, probably going to that gypsy camp judging from the way she was dressed.

Jennifer got out her portfolio of blank, eight-stave paper and climbed into bed. The beat was insistent; the notes were revealing themselves in musical bars, phrases, and movements, like inflections in speech. The dissonance was strong and restless. Rapidly she began writing down the notes.

* * *

Mackenzie pulled the feather pillow over her face and giggled. Dara was already asleep, and Jennifer was writing musical notes.

Alfonso had told them a little about himself. He had worked as the rector's administrative assistant for one year. Before that, he was a student at the university. Dara had been right to think he was originally from one of the islands. Like the Granchellis, he came from a large family. She wondered what kind of fish his dad caught, and what kind of crafts his mother made. Maybe she would get a chance to ask him tomorrow. Of course, Dara would have to translate.

She giggled again and softly repeated his name several times so she could get the final syllable perfect. He was just so nice. Everyone was. She had never felt so much love.

Her mind switched gears to what they had accomplished that day. She had found a couple of loosely-bound notebooks that looked promising. Tomorrow she would take the copy of the Voynich and Carolina's page with her so she could compare them with what she had found. There were definite similarities; the mathematical quotients were similar, as was the sequence of letters that she had identified as part of a sophisticated cryptosystem.

What if Carolina's page turned out to be both significant and valuable? What if they discovered that Carolina was descended from an ancient gypsy tribe, and she was the only surviving ruler? A princess even? Maybe she and Carolina were related. After all, no one knew where she had been born or who her parents were.

But then, the game stopped. That was where it always stopped, because Mackenzie simply couldn't bring herself to think beyond that point. With no more what ifs, she turned on her side, telling herself it didn't matter. Soon she would be graduating from Wood Rose and moving on to bigger and better things. The MIT research program was one of the best in the nation. She just wished she didn't have to leave Carolina and the other FIGs to go there. What if Carolina got a job there? And Dara and Jennifer were there? What if ...

And then she fell asleep.

* * *

Larry punched his feather pillow into a ball and flopped back. He probably should tell Carolina that he was in Frascati, but he knew if he did, she wouldn't feel free to do whatever she needed to do. She would worry about him. No. She needed to do this on her own with as little interference from him as possible. He would tell her later after he had a chance to investigate some things.

The head of the department where he taught wasn't very happy when he told him he needed to take some time off, especially during exams. But his graduate assistant could easily take over his classes. He had done the right thing coming to Frascati. At least he could remain objective. He wasn't sure Carolina could. Then, once she learned the truth, he would be there for her—if she even wanted him. It was risky, he knew, but he had been waiting a long time already. She would either come to terms with her past and move on—with him—or stay lost in some sort of cursed gypsy warp zone. If he had anything to do with it, she would move on and the two of them would build a life together.

His contacts had already confirmed the gypsy woman he had been watching was Carolina's mother. Apparently, the father had died when she was a baby. The death certificate had stated influenza as the cause of death. Oddly enough, he had worked on and off at the Villa Mondragone whenever the tribe traveled to Frascati and made camp nearby. That might explain the special paper Carolina had. Either her father had stolen it, or it had been given to him. He doubted the latter. Normally ancient documents with value weren't split up to give away. It was much more likely that he stole it, knowing it was of value, and that was why it was included in Carolina's *pariktil*. Sort of an insurance policy.

Larry also managed to get some information on the background of Lucia De Rossa, head of the adoption agency. She was 60 years old, and she had lived in Frascati all her life. Her husband ran a small bakery. She hadn't been working at the agency very long when Carolina was adopted. The head of the agency, a man named Liruso, had actually arranged the adoption, but Senora De Rossa might have been involved when Carolina was first taken. Because Liruso believed that Carolina was one of the stolen children, he tried, unsuccessfully, to locate her natural parents. Then, concerned about the gypsies and what they could do if Carolina was placed with an Italian family, he contacted a private agency in the United States and arranged for a couple by the name of Branson to adopt her. Liruso died shortly after that.

Pretty much all of it was straightforward. The story was a familiar one. Carolina's parents were black gypsies, and because Carolina didn't fit the gypsy profile, she had been taken by the State agency and put up for adoption. These things happened, and continued to happen today wherever gypsies camped. The only thing that remained a mystery was Carolina's manuscript page. If she could just find out what that was all about, then maybe, just maybe …

He sat up and pummeled the pillow again. From what his sources had told him, the gypsies had set up camp only a few days before Carolina and the FIGs arrived. So far, Carolina had spent all of her time either at the Granchelli farm or the Old Villa. He was sure Carolina wasn't aware her mother was so near. He had made it a point to meet Mrs. Lovel, and there wasn't any doubt—she was the real thing. A true *choovihni*. Carolina had inherited her mother's strong instincts, possibly other natural gifts as well.

He would talk to Mrs. Lovel again. She was the only one who could give him the answers he needed. Then he would know how best to help Carolina.

Chapter Sixteen

There was one other time in Lyuba's memory when the signs had been dark and conflicted. That was when her loving husband, Balo, came down with the sickness and died. Days later, her beautiful child was taken from her. Now, once again, the signs were black and evil and crossed. She had nothing left to give except her knowledge. Was that it? Did her knowledge of life and healing have to be sacrificed? But how could that be? She had used her knowledge to do good, just as it had been passed down to her by her mother, and her mother's mother. It was what she was born to do.

And then she remembered. The one time she went against all instinct, all knowledge. The one time she allowed the forces of evil to overtake all that she knew to be right and good. A man had died—the man responsible for taking her child.

Lyuba sighed. So it had come full circle, as all things did, and now she must pay for her one transgression. With heavy heart, she gathered her herbs and oils, her crystal, and Tarot cards. She would spend another day in Frascati, but it would be at the mercy of *zee*.

Milosh watched Lyuba leave her hut and walk toward the village. His father had left in the darkness of night, and his mother had gone that morning in the truck. He went back inside the trailer and searched under his bed until he found the jar. Angrily, he shook the jar, once again mixing the contents of ephedra, flitwort, and hair. The tingling sensation he felt in his hands and arms was stronger this time but, unlike before, this time it also spread to his torso. The curse was working.

* * *

With more effort than usual, Carolina got up and dressed. The FIGs had already eaten breakfast by the time she got downstairs.

"My daughter," Mother Granchelli greeted her. She hugged the young woman and felt her forehead. "You feel warm. Perhaps you should stay here and rest today."

"I am fine, Mother Granchelli, really. I am still getting over the flight. It's just jetlag. I'll be all right."

Jennifer poured Carolina a cup of black coffee, and Mackenzie served her a plate of pancakes that she had made. "Jennifer made the coffee this morning," she told Carolina.

"It's the first time I have ever made coffee," Jennifer admitted. "So it might not taste good."

Carolina smiled and sipped the hot black liquid. "You are a natural chef. It is perfect—just strong enough." She began picking at the pancakes. "Mackenzie, these are delicious. I'm just not very hungry."

Mother Granchelli shook her head in disapproval. "Tonight you will eat my *zuppa di primavera,* which the girls helped me make." She couldn't bring herself to call these three beautiful girls FIGs. Figs were a fruit, not her children. "It will make you feel better."

When they arrived at the villa, Alfonso had a pot of fresh black coffee, a sugar bowl and creamer, and some hard rolls ready for them in case they got hungry. Dara immediately went to the manuscript she had pulled from the shelves. From what she found out about the gypsy language, there was no question in her mind that the material was written in Romany. She compared each of the pages. Not all of them were from the same time period, but they each had been written in the same hand.

"What did you find, Dara?" Jennifer sat down next to her with some hand-drawn illustrations she had discovered. Mackenzie and Carolina stopped what they were doing as well.

"I just can't get over the feeling that what we are trying to identify is associated with gypsies. Basically, gypsies use the Indo-European family of languages that comprises the mother tongue of Romany. Within that family are several dialectal sub-groups that include Vedic Sanskrit, which is the language of the most ancient extant scriptures of Hinduism. Grammatically, Sanskrit has eight cases for the noun, three genders, and three voices for the verb. Then there is the subfamily of Indo-Iranian, which consists of three groups of languages, the Dardic, the Indic, and the Iranian. To complicate things even more, gypsies were known to borrow considerable vocabulary from the languages of people they came in contact with. I think some these pages, and Carolina's special page, is a combination of the various sub-groups and perhaps borrowed vocabulary. That is why it is so difficult to pin down. With so many different sources, many of which no longer exist, it is hard to associate what might be gypsy writings with an already established language."

Mackenzie handed Dara the loose-bound notebooks she had discovered the day before. "These look like they are part of the same manuscript."

Dara looked up and smiled. "I believe what we have here, and what Carolina has, is probably the only known gypsy literature in existence. Do you realize what that means? There has never been any important literature in Romany except for some biblical translations where the Roman and Cyrillic alphabets were used. These pages are definitely a written history of a group of gypsies called the *Kaulo Camloes,* which also translates to "Black Comelies." All three FIGs looked at Carolina.

"And, not only that, like the Voynich Manuscript, it has been written in sections. In addition to the section on the history of the *Kaulo Camloes*, there are sections on medicinals, religion, botanicals, astrology and astronomy, cures, and curses."

"Just like the Voynich," said Jennifer.

Mackenzie pulled out her copy of Carolina's page, which she had brought with her, and handed it to Dara. "Look, it is the same handwriting as what is on these library documents. Carolina's page isn't a history, though. It seems to be a letter."

Carolina sat down, her head spinning. "Can you make out any of the script, Dara?"

"I recognize some of the words in Sanskrit. Daughter, love, beautiful ..." Dara grew quiet. "Carolina, it is a letter from your father. He must have written it right after you were born."

Mackenzie started sobbing, and when she did, Jennifer put her arm around her, flipping her ponytail as she did. Dara remained stoic. "It is just so nice," Mackenzie managed to choke out between sniffles.

For the next several hours, Carolina and the FIGs looked through the other materials removed from the shelves to see if there was anything similar to what they had already discovered. There was nothing else.

"I just don't understand." Carolina leaned back in a chair, her stomach feeling a little queasy. She reached for a roll and nibbled on it. "If all of this was written by the same person who wrote the letter to me, and that person was my father, then that must mean my father is responsible for writing this gypsy literature." She looked up at the FIGs. "Is that how you figure it?"

All three nodded. "He had to be well educated," said Jennifer, flipping her ponytail.

"Maybe he worked at the villa," suggested Mackenzie, her problem-solving skills kicking in.

"That's it," said Dara. "Alfonso told us

yesterday that the university has always hired its students, but before the university took it over, the Jesuits hired the locals who could read and write, especially to help in the two libraries. They must have hired your dad, Carolina. Come on. We need to check it out with the rector."

The four young women once again found themselves comfortably seated on the purple velvet upholstered antiques. Rector Catoni seemed pleased they had sought him out. Unfortunately, he didn't have the answers to their questions. "I know who might, however," he said smiling broadly.

After a flurry of telephone calls, Senor Guido Fabiani, Jesuit priest and rector emeritus of the university, was located, and he happily accepted Rector Catoni's invitation to join him and four delightful young women for lunch that day at the Old Villa.

Carolina and the FIGs returned to the library. Some of the material they had examined didn't have any connection to the main body of works they had uncovered, so they returned it to the shelves where it had been found. Even then, the sheer amount of work that had been written by one person was enormous. "Two hundred pages," Mackenzie counted.

"The illustrations are similar to the Voynich

as well," said Jennifer, looking at the colorful sheets spread out in front of her.

Meanwhile, Dara was busy translating Carolina's page and writing it out in English. It was just as they had said; it was a written expression of love to a daughter from her father.

* * *

Larry knew where he would find Mrs. Lovel. He had been observing her for several days and was familiar with her routine. He stood in the doorway of the government building and waited. She would come soon.

Within minutes, she arrived at her favorite place, and spread out her cloth in the shade of the large maple. If she realized he was nearby, she didn't indicate it. Instead, she concentrated on arranging her bags of dried herbs, the jars of creams and ointments, and bottles of oil for display, taking her time, making sure everything was exactly just so.

"Mrs. Lovel."

She looked up quickly. She hadn't known he was nearby.

"Ah, my American friend. You wish another reading from the Tarot?"

She recovered quickly.

He removed another 100,000 lire note from his pocket and placed it on her spread. "I have questions that only you can answer."

The *zee* presented itself in many shapes and forms. Lyuba knew them all; she knew when to feel fear, when to feel sadness, and when to feel happiness. This young man did not threaten. There was also no need to be sad. Yet there was something mysterious about him. Somehow he was connected to her.

Like before, she motioned for him to sit across from her. She would answer his questions.

"You have questions about love, perhaps? Fortune?" She knew he wished to discuss neither with her.

"Mrs. Lovel, I know your daughter."

In all her years as a *choovihni,* she had never been surprised by what the human mind was capable of. Nor had she been surprised by the actions or words of man. This young man, however, had left her breathless. She knew he spoke the truth.

Before she could say anything, he continued. "You see, I love your daughter. I want to marry her. I want us to spend the rest of our lives together."

Lyuba listened. "I hear what you want; what does my daughter want?"

Larry glanced away for a moment. "She wants

to find out who she is, who you are, and the meaning of her inheritance. For without that knowledge, she can't be whole. She can't live a fulfilled life. These questions haunt her."

Lyuba's eyes glistened. Her precious child. Now a grown woman. "Tell me about my daughter," her words barely a whisper.

And Larry did. He told the gypsy woman how they had met, all the things they shared, the strong bond they had, the respect, the love. He told her about Carolina's accomplishments, the FIGs and Wood Rose. And he told her about the wonderful woman her daughter had become; her intelligence, her love for all things, her strong instincts especially when it involved people, and her understanding of nature. "She has inherited the gift," said Larry. "She hasn't learned how to use it because she doesn't realize she even has it. But, like you, she is a *choovihni*."

Lyuba was surprised this man knew the term. "And how do you know this?"

"Because I am the son of a Gypsy King."

The statement was without false pride; it was merely to inform.

Lyuba reached for his hand and searched the palm. The star was present. She touched it with her index finger. He told the truth.

"Unlike Carolina, I chose to leave the tribe. Carolina wasn't allowed to make that choice. That is what needs to be resolved."

Lyuba nodded. This was part of the reason for the conflicting signs.

The two of them spent the morning together— the gypsy woman and the man who loved her daughter. There was much to say.

Chapter Seventeen

Bakro was small for his age, but what he lacked in size he made up for with a loving nature and determination. An only child, he wished to please. His reward was knowing that his actions gave others happiness. His mother was proud of her little boy. He was a good child, even tempered and obedient. So when Bakro suddenly began to behave in wicked ways, she became concerned. Never had Bakro tried to hurt the animals, yet he had been caught whipping a dog for no apparent reason. Mean spirited. He was also seen dumping the container of milk that had been put aside for cooking. Wasteful. Always polite, he was now argumentative and hurtful with his words.

Other mothers were complaining about their children's bad deeds as well. At first whispers passed between friends; then warnings spread throughout the camp. Something evil was taking over the souls of the *Kaulo Camio* children. The *choovihni* needed to be made aware so she could protect them.

After two days of putting up with her son's foul mouth and misconduct, Rupa had enough. Only one person could be responsible for influencing her son in such a negative way, and that person was Milosh.

Djidjo had stayed behind that morning, deciding not to go into the village with the other women. Rupa waited until she was sure Djidjo was alone, then went to the trailer. This would be the last time she would appeal to Djidjo. If she didn't do something about her son, then Rupa would go directly to the Bandoleer.

* * *

"Do Italians always eat so much?" Carolina stared in amazement at the luncheon that had been prepared for them at such short notice.

The rector laughed. "This is a special occasion. Not often do we have such distinguished visitors at the villa."

They were in the main dining room. The rector had thoughtfully arranged for Senor Guido Fabiani and Carolina to be seated next to one another. An elderly gentleman, the retired Jesuit priest with soft white hair spoke with a surprisingly strong voice. His pleasure at being invited to the villa for lunch was obvious.

After the initial introductions and polite comments of triviality were behind them, they began discussing what was foremost in the minds of Carolina and the FIGs. Senor Fabiani was more than willing to tell them everything he remembered.

"Back then, of course, there weren't that many who could both read and write," he explained. "The priests could manage adequately, but once the fund belonging to the Collegio Romano was transferred to the villa, the work became overwhelming."

"Fund is what the private library collections were called," explained the rector, "and the Voynich Manuscript was included in that fund."

"That was when we started looking for additional help outside the villa. There were some people who came to work a few hours each day, sorting and cataloging."

"Did you ever hire gypsies?" asked Dara, who was always the first to bring to light the topic that was foremost in their minds.

The priest cocked his head in thought, trying to remember. "Strange you should ask." He had remembered.

Carolina could hardly breathe. The FIGs sat

motionless, waiting. Only the rector continued to eat.

"There was a gypsy who traveled this way with his tribe usually in the spring—about this time of the year. Such a smart man. His name was ... let me think. Balo! That's it. His name was Balo Lovel." Oblivious to the mounting emotions surrounding him, he continued. "Balo was like a scribe for his tribe, the *Kaulo Camioes,* the Black Comelies. A kind, thoughtful man, and well educated. He was responsible for cataloging all of the materials in the *Bibliotheca Secreta* and recording the information. He always signed his name to each record so that if a question were to arise, we would know where the information had come from. In fact, most of what was completed, he was responsible for. He helped us a great deal over the years until he suddenly died. There was a flu epidemic that year, you see."

Carolina gasped. Her father was dead. She didn't even remember him, yet knowing that he was dead left her feeling sad and emotionally drained. Jennifer reached across the table and poured more wine into Carolina's glass. "Sip that, Carolina." Dara and Mackenzie watched her with concern.

Senor Fabiani stopped talking long enough to refill his plate. It had been a while since he had enjoyed being the center of attention. Most people found his stories tiring.

Carolina took several deep breaths and several sips of wine. Both helped calm her nerves. She removed one of the sheets they had discovered in the library and handed it to the retired rector. "Do you recognize this?"

Senor Fabiani adjusted his glasses and examined the single page. After a while, he pointed to the small initials at the bottom of one corner. "Yes, this is something Balo wrote, although I don't recognize the document. It has his initials, though, and it is in his handwriting."

Rector Cantoni, sensing that something significant was happening but not knowing exactly what, refilled his guests' wine glasses. The priest nodded in appreciation and continued to talk.

"He brought his young daughter to meet us one time." The priest smiled, remembering. "Such a pretty little thing—nothing like her father. He was dark-skinned, you see. All of the *Kaulo Camioes* were. She was fair-skinned, with great big green eyes, and so smart. I'll never forget, she carried on a conversation like an adult. We spent some time in the garden, and I was amazed that she knew the names of all the plants. Such a little thing, with such big words coming out of her mouth. Balo said her mother had taught her. She was the *choovihni* for the tribe, which is someone much like the shaman in your Native American Indian tribes."

Senor Fabiani glanced over at Carolina and paused, then adjusted his eye glasses. "*Dei Mater alma!*" He adjusted his glasses again as the reality of the situation presented itself. "You are that child! You are the child of Balo, aren't you?"

But Carolina didn't answer. She didn't hear the question. She only felt the heat, and then not even that. Losing consciousness, she slumped over into the arms of the startled elderly priest.

* * *

Mrs. Lovel had been able to tell him most of the things he needed to know. All of the pieces of Carolina's past were in place except for one: the special page, which had been given to her in her *parik-til*. "That was a gift to Carolina from her father," Mrs. Lovel told Larry. "I don't know its significance other than it was something he wanted her to have." If Larry could find out what it was—he prayed it wasn't something stolen—then Carolina would finally be free from her past.

Larry dressed in full britches, the full-sleeved white blouse, and boots. As a final touch, he tied the scarf around his neck, the red one, indicating an occasion of celebration. It had been a long time since he had seen him, but he knew he would be expecting him. He would receive Larry, and Larry would again respectfully ask for his help.

Chapter Eighteen

Lyuba returned on the road to camp, her heart overflowing with joy. At last she knew her precious daughter was all right. Her daughter's young man, Larry, had told her so many things— things that made her happy. Now, no matter what, she could live her life in peace knowing her daughter was well, loved, and cared for.

A single magpie landed on a tree branch above her head—a warning. Just outside the camp, she paused, listening. The women were angry. Something had happened.

She approached the clearing and joined the group of women where Rupa was shouting accusations against Milosh. "He is the cause of our trouble." Several other women, all mothers of young children, agreed. "I have warned Djidjo, but she chooses not to listen. I have warned the Bandoleer, but he chooses not to listen. Now we have no choice but to call the *kris*."

Lyuba stepped forward. "What has happened?"

Several women began speaking at once. Lyuba understood, even though the confusion of their words made no sense. They believed Milosh had deliberately caused harm to other gypsies, the young children of the *Kaulo Camioes*.

"There can be no *kris* unless you have proof," she explained. "Do you have proof?"

"Of course not." Milosh stepped forward out of the shadows where he had been lurking. "There is no proof because I haven't done anything. Just ask the kids."

Lyuba heard the falsehood in his words, she saw the blackness of his heart, and it pained her. What the women were saying was true. He had tried to harm the young ones. Still, until one of the children stepped forward and admitted it, they could not hold the *kris*.

"I will speak to the Bandoleer," said Lyuba. "Now, all of you must go and tend to your own business."

One by one the women returned to their homes. After all, Lyuba was the *choovihni*, the wise woman. She knew what was best.

* * *

The sweet and gentle disposition of Mother Granchelli suddenly turned to that of a foreign dictator when Rector Catoni and Alfonso showed up carrying Carolina, the FIGs flitting around their friend like frightened chicks.

"Papa, call that doctor in the village," she ordered, as she scurried ahead of the others to prepare Carolina's bed. "I knew she should stay here today and rest," she said to no one in particular. Clucking her tongue, she expertly pulled down the spreads and sheets where the two men could lay the unconscious woman. "Mackenzie, get a pot from the kitchen and fill it with the ice from the freezer in the basement. Jennifer, go to the bathroom and wet a clean cloth. Use cold water. Dara, you check on Papa; make sure he tells the doctor to come quickly." Everyone scattered.

Not knowing what else to do, the rector and Alfonso went back downstairs to wait for the doctor. They had never seen a woman faint before—and the entire ordeal had frightened them. Senor Fabiani practically had a heart attack when he suddenly found himself holding Carolina. He quickly left, so as not to be in the way, but not before securing the promise from both Rector Catoni and Alfonso that they would let him know how the poor young woman got along.

Dr. Troyano appeared within minutes, since he had been lunching nearby. With both Papa and Dara answering his questions, he had a fairly good picture of what had taken place before his arrival. What he didn't know was the reason for Carolina's collapse. Probably, the young woman had just gotten a little overly heated.

The first thing he did was tell everyone to leave the room, except for Mother Granchelli. After all, it was her home, and he might need her assistance. She explained how Carolina had appeared pale for the past couple of days, had not been eating well, had been feeling a little warm, and had looked generally run down. No, she didn't think it was something she ate, "certainly nothing that I have cooked," she told him with a little more firmness than she intended when he asked. She had been cooking since ever since she was a young girl, and never had anyone gotten sick. The very idea!

The doctor did all of the usual things, checking her blood pressure, pulse, and temperature, which was extremely high. He immediately ordered bags of ice to be put around her to cool her body. A fan would help. He also took a small sample of blood, which he would get tested back at the lab. Other than that, and until the results came back from the lab, there was nothing else he could do.

"There, there," he cajoled Mother Granchelli, who was wringing her hands in her apron. "It will be all right. She is a young, strong woman. It is probably just a virus of some sort."

But Mother Granchelli knew better. She had raised five children and 11 grandchildren. She herself had been the oldest in a large family of nine. She knew all the signs and symptoms of illnesses, and what to do for them. This was different, however. It was much more insidious. And it frightened her. It also frightened the FIGs.

* * *

Dara, Mackenzie, and Jennifer took turns throughout the remainder of the day and night putting fresh icepacks around Carolina's body and adjusting the small fan Papa had found hidden in the attic. It didn't seem to be doing any good. The doctor called early the next morning to say that nothing unusual showed up in the lab results. He would come out later that morning to check on his patient. When he did come, he took another sample of blood for additional tests. In the meantime, all he could do was suggest more icepacks. "If she doesn't get better by tomorrow, we'll have to move her to the hospital," he said on the way out.

After he left, Mother Granchelli insisted the FIGs eat breakfast. She wasn't about to let them lose their strength and get sick as well.

"We need to do something," said Dara as they sat staring at the mountain of scrambled eggs, *copicollo* ham, toast, and grape jelly Mother Granchelli placed in front of them.

Mackenzie, quick at solving problems, agreed. "We need to go visit that gypsy camp and see if anyone there knows Carolina's mother. The priest said she was a *choovihni*. That means she might know how to cure Carolina."

"And if no one knows her, then maybe there is someone else who will help," suggested Jennifer. "Maybe there will be another *choovihni* around."

The girls quickly finished breakfast and cleaned up. After checking on Carolina, making sure there was plenty of ice around her and the fan was turning just so, they left the farmhouse and walked across the field toward the gypsy camp. Within minutes they came to the clearing. Dogs barked at them and young children ran up to stare. The camp itself consisted of several small trailers, a few tents, and some huts. One of the huts was larger than the others, and it had a lean-to. They looked around for an adult, but only saw a boy who looked to be about their age. He had come from one of the trailers and looked like he had just gotten out of bed. "It's still early; maybe gypsies sleep late," said Mackenzie.

Dara, being the most outspoken of the three FIGs, went over to where the boy was standing. His hands were on his hips, and his dark eyes showed distrust.

"I was wondering if you could help us," said Dara.

He glared at her, then at Mackenzie and Jennifer. "What do you want?"

The resentment was obvious. They were intruders.

"We are looking for Mrs. Lovel."

"She's a *choovihni*," said Mackenzie trying to be helpful. Her lisp was pronounced.

"Is that so? And what do you want with *Mrs. Lovel*?"

Dara didn't like his attitude or his tone of voice, and she, for one, wasn't going to put up with it, gypsy or not.

"Listen, punk, just tell us if Mrs. Lovel is here." She raised her form to its full height of five feet eight inches, a good three inches taller than the surly boy, and her dark eyes locked onto his.

He clenched his fists. How dare this stranger

come into his camp and demand information. "Do you know who you are talking to?"

"I know that you either got up on the wrong side of the bed, or you are just naturally rude."

Hearing voices in disharmony, Lyuba opened her door and stepped out into the soft morning light. She was startled to see three young women—strangers—in confrontation with Milosh. After a brief moment, she also realized who they were. They were the three FIGs Larry had spoken of the day before. The smart young women her daughter was teaching.

She hurried to them. Something was wrong for them to come into the camp. "I am Lyuba. Can I help you?"

Dara frowned at the boy with the bad case of ill manners and turned her attention to the woman. "We are sorry to intrude like this, but we are looking for Mrs. Lovel. It really is important." Jennifer and Mackenzie nodded.

"Come." Lyuba led the three girls to her hut, the one with the lean-to, away from Milosh and other prying eyes.

The hut was small, but comfortable and clean. There was a strong, fresh scent of herbs. "It smells a little like Carolina's bungalow," whispered Jennifer. The FIGs sat close to each other on a day bed covered with a spread, not saying anything, and watched the woman, supposedly Carolina's mother, prepare a pot of hot herbal tea. They had only seen the one photograph Carolina had, and it had been taken years earlier, but this gypsy was definitely the woman in that photograph. They could tell by the high cheek bones and especially the eyes. She also wore her hair in the same way—pulled straight back off her face and twisted in a bun at the nape of her neck.

When the tea was ready, the gypsy served them. "I am Lyuba Lovel," she said. "Tell me what is wrong."

Mackenzie and Jennifer looked at Dara. She would explain it to this gypsy—the mother of Carolina. And she did. She told her how they had come to Frascati to find out about Carolina's parents and her adoption. "And to discover the meaning of a special page she was given by her birth parents," added Mackenzie, "or to be more exact, her father." Then Dara told her how Carolina had suddenly gotten sick, and the doctor couldn't find out what was wrong. Now she had a high fever and they were using ice and a fan but she wouldn't wake up, and she might have to go to the hospital, and everything was terrible, and—just then Dara started to cry. It came from somewhere so deep and dark, and so hidden away, that not even she knew it was there. Never in her life had she cried, not even when as a small child she had gone hungry. Not even when her mother left her at the store and never came back. Not even all those times at the orphanage when she felt so alone and afraid.

It frightened Jennifer and Mackenzie to see their friend in so much distress. They moved closer to her. "It will be all right," said Jennifer. She put her arm around Dara. "We will take her to a doctor in Rome if we have to," said Mackenzie, trying to come up with a solution. "They will have better doctors there."

Lyuba watched and listened, then quickly gathered several bags of herbs and bottles of extracts. "Take me to her," she told them. Milosh and several other *Kaulo Camioes* watched Lyuba hastily depart the camp, not knowing that the three young settlers with her were females of intellectual genius.

* * *

The crows gave warning first, then the starlings. The dogs were the last to give notice to the travelers that a stranger was approaching. By the time Larry arrived at the camp, everyone knew he was coming. And because there is a protocol, even among the travelers, the Gypsy King waited until permission was sought before greeting his son.

A tall man, at least for a gypsy, with a straight

and muscular build, his gray hair pulled straight back and secured at the nape of his neck with a scrap of red ribbon, the Gypsy King moved out into the open and embraced his only son. He openly wept, for it had been too long, and he felt no shame in showing his love for this one who had followed his own conscience. Many observed the reunion, but no one spoke. That would come later, in the evening, with food, dance, and song.

The Gypsy King led his son into his home, a trailer slightly newer and a little larger than the others, where he lived alone as a widower. The two men had so much to talk about, yet at that moment, neither could speak. They would take their time, let the subjects present themselves, until whatever distance had developed between them during the separation was no longer present.

Larry came to show respect and love for his father, and to ask for his father's help. He would have known Carolina's parents; as the Gypsy King, he knew all the gypsies of the various tribes in the region. He would also know if Carolina's father had been a thief.

For now, however, it was the love and respect for his father that was foremost in Larry's mind. The questions would come later.

Chapter Nineteen

M ilosh strutted around camp, making threatening gestures toward the young children playing, laughing at their obvious fear of him. His mother had gone on the truck into the village, and his father hadn't returned yet from his trip. The son of the Bandoleer was on his own. He could do anything he pleased, and no one was around to stop him.

What had those three girls wanted with Lyuba? And what was Lyuba doing helping settlers? He would have to discuss this with his father when he returned.

Bored, with nothing to do, he went inside the trailer and found the jar. The last time he had shaken it, he felt the electric tingling in his torso as well as his arms. This time he shook it extra hard and then tossed it under his bed. The shock took his breath as it coursed through his entire body and he had to sit down. He wondered if the three girls had anything to do with that photograph in Lyuba's hut. Maybe that was why they had come searching for her.

* * *

Lucia hadn't slept well for several nights now and she knew why. Until she confessed to Carolina her role in Carolina's abduction, for that is what it was, and then the adoption, she would never feel at peace again. Today she would find the right moment to talk to Carolina in private. Lucia still was uncertain whether she should tell Carolina she had seen her mother only recently. Considering it, she decided she would just wait and see how things went.

After leaving word at her office that she wouldn't be in, she put on her favorite dress to build her confidence, the one with red and yellow flowers and tiny buttons down the front. More than likely Carolina and the FIGs were already at the villa working in the *Bibliotheca Secreta*, but Mother Granchelli had invited her to have lunch with them. She would go to the farmhouse and help Mother Granchelli prepare the meal and wait for Carolina and the FIGs to return.

She picked up her purse and car keys, then,

as a final thought, she went back into her bedroom. There on top of her dresser was the *parik-til* Carolina's mother had given her. She pressed it to her lips, smelling its sweet scent, and then pushed it into her bra. It would bring her good luck.

Since she had plenty of time, she would stop at the bakery. Before leaving early that morning, her husband had told her he was baking some *granciambellone* sweet bread. She would take a fresh loaf to Mother Granchelli. Maybe some nice *zeppole* as well. Carolina and the FIGs would like that for their dessert.

By late morning, Lucia had a bag of *zeppole*, the *granciambellone*, and several other loaves of assorted Italian breads, telling herself that Mother Granchelli could always use them if Carolina and the FIGs didn't like them. She left downtown Frascati and headed into the country toward the farm. It was such a beautiful day. Too beautiful for Carolina and the FIGs to be closed up in that musty old library, she thought.

She turned onto the driveway leading to the farmhouse, and in a few minutes wheeled into the gravel parking area where she proceeded to unload her packages. Just as she closed the trunk to her car, she saw the three FIGs hurrying across the field toward her. The gypsy woman—Carolina's mother—

was with them. The gypsy woman saw her but said nothing. Automatically, Lucia reached for her *parik-til.*

Jennifer ran ahead to tell Lucia what had happened while Dara and Mackenzie took Lyuba into the house and up the stairs. What had started out to be such a glorious day suddenly turned dark and ugly. Lucia carried her bakery goods into the kitchen where she found Mother Granchelli sitting at the kitchen table staring into a cup of black coffee. When she saw Lucia, she stood up and embraced her. Unable to do anything else, the two women waited together in the kitchen, praying over their rosaries; praying to the patron saint of illness, Mary Magdalen of Pazzi; and praying to Marie Bagnesi, the patron saint of illness and lost parents just for good measure.

* * *

After spending the night, Larry left in the darkness of pre-dawn. He and the Gypsy King had talked deep into the night. Now it was again time for him to leave. He had accomplished what he set out to do. The bond between him and his father had once again been renewed and strengthened, and, he had learned about Carolina's mother and father.

Lighthearted and filled with joy, he drove along the highway toward Frascati. Now he could let Carolina know he was in Frascati. He could also give her the information she needed concerning her parents. And he could tell her about himself. He had kept it from her for too long. Now, with his father's blessing, there was nothing to keep him from telling her the truth.

Streaks of pink and gray light splashed across the eastern sky as the sun began its slow ascent. Larry allowed his thoughts to meander—the deep love he had for Carolina, and the bright future they would have together. Impatiently, he urged the car to go faster. Now that he knew, he wanted to tell Carolina as soon as possible.

Chapter Twenty

"*A*mari *Develeskeridaj*, Our Mother of God," said Lyuba when she saw her daughter. "What has he done to you?" Dara, Mackenzie, and Jennifer sat on the floor against the wall, far enough to be out of the way, but close enough to be near. The rock in Jennifer's chest had gotten large again, and the cadence was dissonant and loud—*fortissimo*—even clashing, suggesting a child's terror. She didn't need to write down the notes; she knew them by heart now—each note, each phrase, each movement. She folded her arms tight against her, trying to ease the pain.

Lyuba pulled out several bags of dried herbs and began mixing them into the oils she had brought with her. "Bring me a small spoon," she said. Mackenzie ran down to the kitchen and quickly returned. It took all four of them, Lyuba and the FIGs, but eventually they got some of the concoction into Carolina's mouth. Then they waited. After a while, Lyuba prepared tea extracts from the asparagus and olive leaves she had brought with her. Once again the four of them administered the thick liquid, and they waited.

Later, when there still was no change, Lyuba asked for a bowl of egg whites and a clean handkerchief. She soaked the handkerchief in the egg whites and wrapped it around Carolina's feet, but even with this, Carolina's fever didn't break. At some point Mother Granchelli insisted they come downstairs and eat something. Only the gypsy woman stayed behind, not wanting to leave her precious daughter alone.

When nightfall approached, and there was no change in Carolina's condition, the gypsy woman packed up her herbs to leave. She saw the panic in the faces of the three young girls, and felt their love for her daughter. "I will return," she said. And she disappeared into the darkness.

Lyuba didn't return to camp. Instead she walked toward Frascati. Larry had told her where he was staying. She needed to find him, the man who loved her daughter. He could help.

She knew who had done this evil thing against her daughter. The missing herbs, the hair taken from the lock of hair she had kept with the photograph; somehow he had learned the curse. And now her daughter might die because of his wicked ways. Well, he would soon learn that he and he alone would be held responsible for his actions. He would pay a heavy price for what he had done.

Even in the darkness, Lyuba was familiar with the streets of Frascati; she had walked them many times. The small hotel where Larry was staying was located on the north side of the village. She went to the front desk and asked that they call his room to let him know she was there. At first the clerk didn't want to disturb his guest, especially at such a late hour. But she was insistent. She would wait until he did. Finally, he called, and after several rings and no answer, she left.

He had gone somewhere, but he was still registered. She would wait for him to return. She found a place where she could see anyone leaving or entering the hotel. Then she sat to wait.

* * *

By the time Lucia left to go home, the doctor had not called back, probably an indication that he had learned nothing else from the lab results. Lucia hugged her cousin and told her she would come back early the next morning to see if there was anything she could do to help.

After spending all day working in the vineyard with his sons, Papa returned to a quiet house and ate a bowl of leftover *zuppa di primavera* and several chunks of Italian bread his wife put in front of him. He hadn't seen her this upset in many years, not since one of their sons got hurt on the tractor and almost lost an arm.

When he finished eating, Mother Granchelli began cooking more soup, this time a pot of *jota*, a bean soup with her special ingredient: pickled turnips. Papa hugged her tightly and stroked her hair. Then he left her to her cooking, knowing that was what she did whenever there was something wrong with one of her children. Nothing else would help.

* * *

Without saying anything, Dara gathered her pillow and one of the soft comforters from her bed and carried it into Carolina's room. Mackenzie and Jennifer followed her. They would sleep in her room that night, keeping the ice packs around her, adjusting the fan. One by one they fixed their make-shift beds on the floor, close to each other, and close to Carolina.

Dara had gotten over her crying outburst, but now she was brimming with anger. She stared up at the tall ceiling, no longer noticing it was the tallest ceiling she had ever seen except for the ceilings at the Villa Mondragone. Now that didn't seem important.

How could this have happened? She just didn't understand. They had been inseparable—Carolina and the FIGs. If Carolina caught something—some sort of disease—then all of them should have caught it. And what had Mrs. Lovel meant when she said, "What has he done to you?" Who was she talking about? Was she talking about some sort of curse? She thought of all the remedies she had tried, using herbs and oils and egg whites. Then she thought of the gypsy camp and that hateful gypsy kid trying to act tough. Could he have done something? Were there more kids like him—ill-tempered and mean?

Maybe she was responsible. After all, she always planned what the FIGs should do, like foiling Dr. Harcourt's office, and pruning his bush. There was also the time they spread bird poop on the handle of his car door. And, of course, those porno magazines they ordered. Maybe Carolina was sick because of the FIGs' silly pranks.

She turned over on her side. Carolina was the closest thing she had to family, besides Mackenzie and Jennifer. She was one of them. If anything happened to her ...

More tears started to fall, this time silently.

* * *

Mackenzie stared up at the ceiling, visualizing a probability equation in one quadrant. Using the Law of Sufficient Reason, all of the statistics just didn't add up. There was nothing, at least nothing they knew about, that could have caused Carolina to suddenly get so sick. It had to be an unknown factor, and she had a feeling Mrs. Lovel knew what that factor was. She only hoped she would also know how to solve it. After all, she was a *choovihni*. Maybe she had even run into this type of thing before. She certainly knew a lot about natural medicines. None of them seemed to be working though. She said she would come back. Maybe she had to get more medicines. If Carolina didn't get better by the next day, though, the doctor was right. She would have to be taken to a hospital in Rome.

But what if the doctors in Rome couldn't find out what was wrong with her? What if she stayed sick? What if ...

Mackenzie reached out and felt for Dara's hand. Finding it, she held on to it, afraid to let it go.

* * *

Jennifer turned her back to Mackenzie and Dara, and squeezed her arms tighter around her pillow. Lying down helped to ease the pain a little; the rock was getting smaller again.

Jennifer now understood the meaning of the cadence: the black and white drawing, the watercolor painting, and the notes. The cadence had at last developed into a concerto for violin, the instrument of gypsies, with a prevailing rhapsodic *leitmotif*. The final movement had revealed itself when they were at the gypsy camp. And now it was complete.

It was a concerto in four movements. The first movement, the *allegro maestoso,* had started when Carolina began teaching them at Wood Rose. The second, quietly flowing movement, *in ruhig fliessender bewegung,* developed with their arrival to the Granchelli farm. The *andante moderato* was the third movement. It was Carolina's special page, the loving letter written to her from her father. Now they were in the final movement—*in tempo des scherzos.* Fast, loud, even cacophonous, shadowed in the key of E flat minor until reaching a resounding resolution and ending in the major key of C, eighth and 16th notes—sounds of joy and triumph.

Jennifer played the violin of each section in her

mind; she listened to each note and noted each rest. Then she played the violin with the full orchestra, with all of the sections blended, each instrument complimenting the other. The result was a musical creation more beautiful than anything Jennifer had ever written. It was the cadence of gypsies; it was the heartbeat of Carolina and the FIGs.

Carolina would be all right—she knew that now. The symphony was finally written, and it was never wrong. Jennifer relaxed her arms, testing to see if the rock was still there. It was gone. Quietly she turned over to face her two friends. "Carolina is going to be all right," she whispered, and, trusting her, they smiled.

* * *

Larry turned into the parking lot reserved for hotel guests. It was late, and more than likely Carolina and the FIGs were already in bed. He would get a good night's sleep, and contact Carolina first thing in the morning. He smiled when he thought about how surprised she would be to see him in Frascati.

As soon as he stepped out of the car, she was there. He had no idea where she had come from.

"Mrs. Lovel, what's wrong?"

"You must come now. Carolina needs you."

Larry drove Lyuba to the gypsy camp and waited for her to gather what she needed from her hut. On the way there, she explained what had taken place. When he was growing up, he had also known a gypsy boy with the darkness—a brown *chakra*—around his heart. Like Milosh, he hurt other gypsies. Because of his transgressions, the *kris* had ruled he be banned from his tribe. Like that boy, Milosh would have to pay the same price for his evil actions. There were no other options.

Once Lyuba had everything she needed, the two of them walked through the brush until they reached the ancient live oak next to the stream. Larry knew what was expected of him. After all, he was the son of the Gypsy King. As a young boy, he had been taught by a *choovihni*. He watched Lyuba make her preparations. Near by, an owl hooted—a good omen.

First she handed him the clean sheet of paper. He wrote on it a blessing for Carolina and then a wish to heal her. Then he wrapped the paper around the small stone that had always been with Lyuba; her good luck charm. Kneeling by the tree he scattered bread and wine, and, finally, water from the nearby spring.

"Tree mother, I feed you; feed me in return." He spoke the spell as though he had learned it only yesterday, not all those years ago as a young boy. "Tree mother, I quench your thirst; quench mine in return." He buried the paper at the base of the tree, saying, finally, "Tree mother, I bring you a gift; bless me in return." He put both hands on the tree. "Rain falls, wind blows, sun shines, grass grows." He repeated it three times and then walked away without looking back.

Larry drove Lyuba back to the gypsy camp, and then, exhausted from worry more than anything else, he returned to the hotel. It would soon be daylight. Until then, there was nothing left to do.

Chapter Twenty One

*M*ilosh was worried. He had overheard the young mothers complaining to his father as soon as he returned. Already tired and irritable, the Bandoleer wasn't in the mood to hear the accusations against his son. His trip had not gone well; he had spent two days negotiating, and still had not gotten the van he wanted. It was an old van with many miles; the tribe couldn't afford anything better. Still, the dealer would not accept his offer. Disappointed, the trip back to camp had made him especially weary. Once he was rested, however, he would hold a meeting, and anyone who had a grievance could speak at that time.

His father had never listened before, but now he had told them he would hold a meeting. This was not good. He had seen it happen another time to another gypsy who had upset the balance of the tribe.

There had been a meeting, and then a *kris*. The gypsy had been forced out of the tribe, never to return. Milosh, however, was the son of the Bandoleer. They couldn't do anything to him—his father wouldn't allow it.

Milosh settled down onto his bed. Behind his head he felt something hard—the jar. He carelessly tossed it to one side. Tomorrow he would get rid of it; it was the only thing that might prove what he had done.

* * *

Larry slept fitfully, then woke just as the sun started to rise. He quickly showered and dressed and drove out to the Granchelli farm. No one was about, so he waited in the car not wanting to disturb anyone. He wondered if Lyuba had gotten any rest. Just then he saw an older man coming from the barn carrying two buckets of fresh milk. Larry climbed out of the car and walked toward him.

"Can I give you a hand with that?" he offered.

Papa looked at Larry and smiled as though he had been expecting him.

"Sure you can," he said. "And who might you be?"

"My name is Larry Gitani. I am a friend of

Carolina's."

Papa's grin got bigger. "I see. You just happened to be in the neighborhood?"

Not realizing Papa was teasing him, he tried to explain. "Actually I arrived from the States a few days ago—on business." This wasn't easy. How could he explain he was trying to help Carolina find out about her parents, and now help her gypsy mother break the curse that had been placed on her?

"Relax, son. I know who you are. Carolina has already told us about you." Papa set down the pales of milk and shook Larry's hand. "Everyone calls me Papa."

He handed one of the pales to Larry and walked toward the house. "Carolina gave us quite a scare, but she is doing much better this morning. Her mother is already with her. Come on in and get some breakfast."

"Did you say Carolina is doing better and that her mother is with her?" Larry wanted to make sure he understood.

"That's right. I'm not sure when her mother got here, but it must have been pretty early. She was already here when I went to milk the cows. Carolina's fever broke sometime during the night. Now she wants some of Mother Granchelli's cooking. Says she is starved. Nothing makes Mother Granchelli happier than to hear one of her children say they are starved."

Larry followed Papa into the kitchen where he got introduced to the other half of the Granchellis. "This is so exciting," said Mother Granchelli as she hustled back and forth between mixing bowls on the counter and frying pans on the stove. "A miracle." She crossed herself and glanced upward, saying another quick prayer to Mary Magdalen of Pazzi, the patron saint of illness, and to Marie Bagnesi, the patron saint of illness and lost parents.

In the midst of cracking an egg into the hot skillet, she paused just long enough to give Larry the once over. "So, you are Carolina's young man?"

He honestly didn't know what to say. He loved Carolina. He wanted to marry her and spend the rest of his life with her. He wasn't sure she wanted the same thing, though.

"She's already showered and dressed—been up for hours. Her mother and the girls are with her. Run on up the stairs and see her while I finish up breakfast."

Larry didn't have to be told a second time. He took the stairs two at a time, peeked into the first room he came to, a cheerful room wallpapered in large yellow roses. It was empty. Following the sound of voices, he walked down the hall to the next room, and there he found her, sitting up in bed, laughing with three young girls who had to be the FIGs, Lyuba, and another woman, whom he guessed was probably Lucia.

"Larry! What are you doing here?" Carolina reached out her arms to hug him.

"You didn't think I was going to let you come to Italy and have all the fun, did you?" He tried to sound light-hearted. He glanced at Lyuba and silently gave thanks. Only the two of them would ever know how close they came to losing Carolina.

"I'm afraid I got a little sick," she explained. "But whatever it was, I seem to be all right now." Then taking Lyuba's hand, she said, "Larry, I want you to meet my mother."

He looked into the face of this gentle and wise gypsy woman who had been born with the special gift. Her unspoken message to him was clear. It would serve no useful purpose for Carolina to know what they had done.

"It is my distinct pleasure," he said. "And I assume these three beautiful young ladies are the infamous FIGs I have heard so much about."

Jennifer poked Mackenzie who immediately giggled. "Infamous," she repeated.

"We won't tell what we have heard about you if you don't tell about what you have heard about us," said Dara.

"That's a deal."

Lucia stood up from where she had been sitting and offered her hand. "I am Lucia De Rossa."

"Yes. Carolina's friend."

The fact that he referred to her as Carolina's friend made Lucia happy.

From the bottom of the stairs Papa yelled that breakfast was on the table. There were a few moments of confusion as everyone wanted to help Carolina negotiate getting out of bed and then navigate the stairs. Eventually, it was Larry who helped her, but not before giving Lucia a quiet moment alone with Carolina. "Would you mind?" she asked Larry. "This won't take long."

"I wanted to tell you before, but there just didn't seem to be the right time." She simply couldn't hold it back any longer. She told Carolina everything she remembered about that horrible day when she was taken from her mother. Lucia mopped her eyes with her handkerchief. "I have carried the guilt all my life."

Carolina had suspected all along that Lucia knew more about what happened. Now she was admitting that she had been there, in the garden, where she was taken from her mother. Carolina didn't remember what happened; she only vaguely remembered things about the garden. "There was nothing else you could do, Lucia. It was your job." Carolina put her arms around her friend. "I don't hold you responsible, so you mustn't either. Anyway, look how it has turned out. I have found my mother. Everything has worked out just as it should."

Larry supported Carolina down the stairs just in case she was still weak and they joined the others in the kitchen. Unlike the day before when the house had been so quiet, now it was once again filled with the joyful sounds of friendship and love.

* * *

Gradually, over Mother Granchelli's enormous breakfast, Carolina and the FIGs told Larry what they had discovered at the villa; that Carolina's father had actually written a history of the *Kaulo Camio* gypsy tribe and left it in the *Bibliotheca Secreta*. "No one even knew it was there." Carolina reached over and pressed Lyuba's hand. "He must have been very smart."

Lyuba had been sitting quietly, only nodding when she was spoken to. She nodded now.

"The interesting part is, what my father wrote was constructed the same way as the Voynich Manuscript, even though his writing was done totally independent of the Voynich. There was no way he could have known about the Voynich or seen it because it had already been sold to Wilfrid M. Voynich. You see the implications. This means that the Voynich Manuscript was more than likely written by a gypsy. Maybe even as early as the eleventh century, back when gypsies were known as land tramps."

"And your special page, Carolina," said Dara. "Tell Larry about your special page."

"Well, Dara was actually able to translate it once we found the other documents my father had written, because it was also written by him. It was a personal letter to me. He must have written it right after I was born."

Lyuba smiled. So like her Balo to do something like that. He had loved his little daughter very much.

Lyuba watched her daughter sharing her happiness with those around her. Her *chaktra* was violet, crowning her head, an indication of psychic power, complete understanding, and fulfillment. She had grown into such a beautiful young woman. She had a bright future with this son of the Gypsy King who was also separated from the tribe. They would do well together. Lyuba placed her hand over her heart; she knew she would have to soon leave. It was the only way. Her daughter had another life now, a life that was not part of the gypsy way. She wished her much happiness, but she would not interfere or hold her back.

After breakfast, Lyuba excused herself. "I must return to camp now," she told the others. "Thank you for your hospitality," she said to Mother Granchelli.

"You are family," she said, hugging the gypsy woman. "You are welcome any time."

Carolina walked outside with her mother; a stranger, yet someone she had known her entire life. "We will have to return to North Carolina in a few days," she said. "Would you like to go with us? The FIGs will be graduating, and then I should be able to get some time off."

The gypsy woman smiled, her heart overflowing with love for her child, and breaking at the same time because she knew she must once again say goodbye. She was not part of Carolina's world. But that wouldn't sever their bond. Nothing could do that.

"Thank you, but not this time." She caressed Carolina on her cheek and touched her silky hair. "We will see each other again," she promised.

The two women embraced each other, neither wanting to say goodbye. Finally, Lyuba turned away and walked toward the gypsy camp, to her people, to where she belonged.

* * *

Later that afternoon Larry drove Carolina and the FIGs to the villa so he could see the documents they had discovered. Carolina also wanted to thank the rector for all he had done for them. "Please tell Rector Fabiani that I apologize for giving him such a fright at lunch the other day."

"His only regret is that he couldn't have spent more time with four such beautiful women." Rector Catoni handed Carolina a package. "He also agreed with me that you should have a copy of your father's manuscript. You will know the right thing to do with it." He kissed Carolina's hand. "Please come back again soon."

Carolina giggled in spite of herself. If the FIGs had been there at that moment, it would have been embarrassing. Instead, Larry took Carolina by her arm and led her out of the massive office decorated in the purple color of royalty and spirituality, ornately-carved antiques, and extremely high ceilings painted in gold leaf.

While the FIGs searched for Alfonso, Carolina and Larry strolled through the villa's gardens. Every so often Carolina would pause, touch a plant or sniff a flower, and tell Larry what its purpose was. Larry watched her, mesmerized. The gift she had inherited from Lyuba was no longer hidden away. Everything that had happened since coming to Frascati had served to unlock her mind once again, allowing the innate knowledge she had been born with to surface.

Carolina sat down on a concrete bench and motioned for Larry to sit next to her. "Now. Tell me why you really came here?" she asked. "Why aren't you at the university giving exams to your students?"

The time had come for Larry to reveal his own hidden past. He told his story of being the son of the Gypsy King, a boy who lost his mother at a young age, and a young man who made the decision to leave the gypsy ways behind to build a future in America. And then he told her how much he loved her and how much he wanted them to share a life together. He told her about all the times he had wanted to tell her, but he knew that until she could reach some sort of resolution with her past, it would be impossible for her to love him. He told her he had come to help her confront her past so he could be with her always.

Afraid to look at Carolina, afraid of what he might see in her eyes, he looked down. She had picked and given him a tiny pink flower, which symbolizes love. It dangled from his fingers.

"I love you, Larry Gitani."

When he heard the words, he thought his chest would explode. Relief, joy, and love flooded his very center of being. "I have always loved you, Carolina. From the first day I saw you when you were lost, running around in circles trying to find out where to register for classes. I will love you until the day I die, and I will even love you after that."

He would have told her more, but the sound of happy giggles alerted them that the FIGs were heading their way. Alfonso was with them.

Chapter Twenty Two

There was still business that needed her attention. Lyuba angrily strolled into camp and went immediately to the Bandoleer's trailer.

"I wish to see Milosh," she said loudly after banging on the door. Several other gypsies came out of their huts and tents to see what was happening.

The Bandoleer opened the door. He had been asleep. "What is it, Lyuba? Why do you come banging on my door?"

Without waiting to be invited, she pushed her way past the Bandoleer into the trailer. Inside she found Milosh cowering on his bed, the jar laying haphazardly in full view next to him. "So, little boy, you think you can play with curses?" She reached over him and snatched up the jar. "This is what your son has been playing with." She held it up for the Bandoleer to see. "It almost cost the life of an innocent one—the life of another gypsy."

A gasp came from Milosh's mother. To harm or even try to harm another gypsy was against the gypsy law. Punishment would be severe. "Please, Lyuba. Don't do this thing."

"I forgave him once, Djidjo, and I warned him. He chose not to listen. Now I demand the *kris*." She looked back at the Bandoleer. "If you are not strong enough to preside, I shall find another, but there will be a *kris*."

The *choovihni* had spoken. Nothing else could be done.

Lyuba left the trailer, taking the jar with her. Satisfied, the other gypsies returned to their own homes. Now, at last, something would be done about Milosh.

* * *

Dara stared up at the tall ceiling, the tallest ceiling she had ever seen except for the ones at the Old Villa, unable to sleep. This would be their last night at the Granchelli's home. She would miss Mother Granchelli and Papa. She had learned much, but most of all, she had learned what it was like to have a real family. She had never known that, even before her mother left.

She was happy for Carolina—finding her mother. The gypsy woman was so different from Carolina—probably like she and her mother would be if she were to find her. Yet they shared a bond of love that would never be broken. She wondered if her own mother still loved her or even thought about her. And, like always, she wondered why her mother left her.

She and the FIGs would soon graduate from Wood Rose and then go their separate ways. But they would never lose touch with one another, or with Carolina. No matter what, they were family, too. Just a little different.

Dara sighed deeply and closed her eyes, the memory of croaking tree frogs and cicadas, and ditch water tickling her feet; *You wait right here, pretty girl. I'll be back ...*

* * *

Mackenzie giggled. She knew Dara and Jennifer weren't asleep yet; she could tell by the way they were breathing. So she didn't put the pillow over her face. She just giggled out loud.

Alfonso said he would write to her at MIT in Cambridge once she got settled. She would like that.

Of course, she would have to learn Italian, but Dara said she would teach her. And Alfonso knew some English, although he got his personal pronouns and verb tenses mixed up sometimes. But at least they could write to each other.

Mother Granchelli had told her she was an excellent cook. Mackenzie knew she wasn't excellent, but it was nice of Mother Granchelli to tell her so.

She would also write to Mother Granchelli and Papa once she learned Italian. They called her their child, and she liked that. No one had ever called her their child before.

Mackenzi's giggles quieted. Ever since she could remember, she had wanted a forever family—a family where she would fit in and be loved. Now she had two. There were the FIGs and Carolina, and there was Mother Granchelli and Papa. She was fortunate. It had taken a while, but she had finally found what she had been searching for all her life.

Mackenzie smiled into the darkness and closed her eyes. A forever family ...

* * *

The Gypsy Cadence was playing in Jennifer's mind. It made her happy; it was her greatest work. Jennifer had changed since coming to Italy with

Carolina and the FIGs. She knew the heavy rock that had caused her so much pain in the past was now gone for good. She could face whatever her future offered and know that she needn't be afraid.

She had watched Carolina and her mother—two women with so little in common other than the fact that they were mother and daughter—related by blood. Yet that one connection was enough to bond them for life. That seemed to be enough for them, and nothing else mattered.

Jennifer looked around the large room with the pretty yellow roses on the walls and scented with fresh white lilacs. She and her parents had that connection as well before they were killed. Maybe that was enough; and knowing that, maybe now she could let them go, but keep whatever love they had shared in her heart.

Content and at peace in the soft sheets and comforter of her bed, Jennifer slowly drifted to sleep, the musical cadence of a violin playing softly in her mind.

* * *

After Carolina and the FIGs promised to visit the Granchellis and Lucia again; after Lucia promised to visit Wood Rose in North Carolina—

but not the Granchellis because they were too old to travel, they said; and after everyone promised everyone they would take care of themselves, Carolina, Larry, and the FIGs finally left the Granchelli farm and headed for Rome where they were scheduled for a flight back to LaGuardia, then Raleigh. First, though, they would make a stop at the gypsy camp. Carolina wanted to see her mother one last time before leaving. When they got there, however, everything was gone. There weren't any trailers, huts, or tents. Nor was there any sign that the gypsies had ever camped there. It was just a field in the shadow of the ancient Villa Mondragone. Carolina remembered Lucia's words: *They will stay until they feel it is no longer beneficial for them to remain. When they feel it is time to leave, they will. One day they will simply be gone.*

Concerned for what Carolina might be feeling, Larry reached for her hand.

"It's all right," she said. "She was here when I most needed her." Carolina looked out across the field toward the gardens that were still a part of the Old Villa, feeling the strong bond of love she and her mother shared—the love that had always been there and always would. They had already said their goodbyes.

Carolina moved closer to the man she loved as

they drove north toward Rome. There were no more secrets now. She found her past and in doing so, had also found her future. She glanced at the FIGs in the back seat. It had been the right thing to do to include them in the search for her own truth. Now, perhaps, each girl would accept her own past and move forward with confidence and self-assurance.

"Sure glad you are driving, Larry," said Dara from the back seat.

"Yeah," giggled Mackenzie. "Carolina almost got us all killed trying to get out of Rome."

"She just likes to drive in circles," added Jennifer laughing.

They were a family. Their bond was love.

Chapter Twenty Three

$\mathcal{D}$r. Harcourt was in a state of hyperbolic angst; graduation exercises tended to do that to him. His dark gray suit looked all right, but somehow he had managed to spill something on his tie—the one with the smidgeon of maroon. Helpless as to what to do about it, he went searching for Mrs. Ball.

"Oh for pity's sake," she said, whipping out some sort of cleaning apparatus that looked like a short, thin dildo. She had been showing signs of contrariness ever since Carolina and the FIGs had returned from Italy, probably an indication of extreme stress over what the FIGs might do in the short time before graduation. In fact, the entire campus seemed to be exuding a palpitating air of agitation, as though in anticipation of something unknown that was yet to come. Within seconds the offensive spot had been removed, and everything was as right as it could be, considering it was graduation day.

All of the board members were in attendance, as well as several leaders in the community. And, of course, Miss Alcott, who had resumed her frequent visits to Wood Rose since Carolina and the FIGs, had returned from their study trip abroad.

There were also a couple of local reporters to cover the happy event, which was especially nice since Dr. Harcourt planned to use the occasion to announce that a State grant as well as a sizeable Federal grant had been awarded to Wood Rose because of the research Carolina and the FIGs completed while on their recent study-abroad mini course.

With all of the student-residents, faculty, staff, board members, Miss Alcott, and community dignitaries seated, the organist, Dr. Hertzog, who headed the music department, began playing the lively processional, "Jesu Joy of Man's Desiring," by J.S. Bach. Ten graduating seniors proudly marched in single file, one by one, down the red carpeted aisle toward the stage to receive their diplomas, including the three FIGs. Each graduate wore the traditional cap and gown in the traditional dark blue school color. Only the tassel on the cap was yellow.

It was one of the largest classes to graduate

from Wood Rose Orphanage and Academy for Young Women, rich in history and strong in academic achievement, wrote one of the reporters. The other reporter, a woman whose beat usually covered society interests in the Raleigh area, wrote: Dressed alike in robes of dark blue, only the individual accomplishments of the 10 young women graduating from Wood Rose distinguished them from each other—with the exception of three of the graduates: one wore her cap backwards, another wore her cap pitched at a severe slant forward, and the third wore her cap secured at an odd right angle over one ear.

Later that evening, with the services behind them, Dara, Mackenzie, and Jennifer sat in Carolina's living room, surrounded by the happy colors of blue, orange, and yellow.

"Do you know what you want to do this summer before you begin your college classes?" Carolina had been concerned about the FIGs and how they would spend their summer. They had been on such a busy schedule, it seemed strange now that it was all coming to an end.

"Larry said he might know someone who can help me find out where my mother is," said Dara.

"Really?" Carolina wasn't expecting that answer, but, thinking about it, it didn't surprise her.

Dara nodded. "She might be in New York."

"I am going to help," said Mackenzie.

"Me too," added Jennifer.

"It won't hurt to try. We have five weeks before we have to report to school," said Mackenzie.

"I have to report a little earlier, but that will only be for a performance at the Lincoln Center," said Jennifer.

"The Gypsy Cadence?" asked Carolina.

"Yes. It's part of the live performing arts series. Then I'll have another week off before I actually start my classes at Juilliard."

"Wow." Carolina thought back to how much help and support they had given her in her own search. She wouldn't have accomplished what she did if it hadn't been for the FIGs.

Actually, she hadn't made any plans for the summer yet. Larry was teaching two summer sessions at the university, so he would be busy. And she had some vacation time coming.

The FIGs looked at her ... waiting.

"Listen, I don't want to intrude, but ..."

"Great," said all three girls at once.

"We were hoping you would want to come." Dara began talking rapidly, as though she couldn't get the words out fast enough. "Larry said his contact has located five women with the same name as my mother. Only two, though, are good possibilities because of their age and the date they arrived at their current addresses, both of which happen to be in New York. We thought we would go there and try to locate them." Dara paused to take a breath.

"Also," said Mackenzie, "we figured since Connecticut isn't that far from New York, you might want to make a stop at the Beinecke Library at Yale University."

"You could show them the copy of your father's manuscript," said Jennifer; "That is, if you want to."

Carolina caught their excitement. She had been wondering if she should go to Connecticut. Maybe now was the time. Carolina smiled and nodded. She would go with the FIGs to New York in search of Dara's mother. How could she not? And then she and the FIGs could visit the Beinecke Library and meet with the head of the rare documents department. It was time, and it was the right thing to do.

* * *

Jimmy Bob slowly made the rounds in his old, beat-up truck, this time not starting with the ivy-covered stone walls on the outer perimeter and circling back to the center, but driving only around the dormitory and administrative building. The

Durham Bulls were in the play-offs, and it was being televised in a delayed broadcast by the local station. He didn't want to miss any of it. Within 15 minutes, he had checked the dormitory and headed back to the administrative building where he had a bag of cheese chips and a canned soft drink waiting. All was quiet and as it should be.

* * *

"Hurry up, he'll be coming back pretty soon!"

Lynda spelled with a "y" Corgill, who was two years behind Dara, Mackenzie, and Jennifer, and had just completed her sophomore year, squeezed the hot glue gun into the door lock of the headmaster's office. Shelby Andrews, her accomplice and the newest resident to be accepted at Wood Rose, stood watch.

"I see the lights of the truck. Hurry! He's coming back! Are you finished?"

Lynda gave the metal apparatus one last squeeze, filling the lock with the quick-drying cement glue guaranteed to harden on contact. "Finished."

In the soft illumination of the crescent moon high overhead, the two girls, barefooted and wearing dark blue pajamas, ran across the lawn crisscrossed by dark, elongated shadows and dampened by night-cooled air to the maintenance shed where they placed the glue gun on the top shelf where it was normally kept. With their task completed, they quickly returned to the dormitory, to the far end from where Ms. Larkins slept, and crawled through the open window. Within minutes they were back in their rooms, in their individual beds, and sound asleep. The sleep of innocent angels.

It would soon be light; and Wood Rose Orphanage and Academy for Young Women would start another day.

The End

Barbara Casey is the author of five award-winning novels and numerous articles, poems, and short stories. In addition to her own writing, she is an editorial consultant and literary agent. She lives on a mountain in northwest Georgia with her husband, her 6-pound Maltese named Hemingway,and Benton, a hound-mix who adopted her.